THE FACE OF DEATH

Brady took a deep breath. He was tempted to bring the Winchester to bear and open fire. But Brady couldn't force himself to do it. He wanted vengeance, but he wasn't an assassin. He wanted to look Gallup in the eye and tell him what he thought of him, tell him why he deserved to die. He wanted Gallup to know it was Dan Brady's bullet that tore through his body. It would be harder that way, riskier too. But that was just the way it had to be.

Brady got to his feet, not caring whether anyone saw him. He climbed into the saddle, keeping the Winchester out, braced against his thighs.

He wanted justice.

And now he was going to get the chance to make it happen . . .

Also by Bill Dugan

TEXAS DRIVE
GUN PLAY AT CROSS CREEK
DUEL ON THE MESA
MADIGAN'S LUCK

BILL DUGAN

Brady's Law

HarperTorch
An Imprint of HarperCollinsPublishers

This is a work of fiction. Names, characters, places, and incidents are products of the author's imagination or are used fictitiously and are not to be construed as real. Any resemblance to actual events, locales, organizations, or persons, living or dead, is entirely coincidental.

HARPERTORCH
An Imprint of HarperCollins*Publishers*
10 East 53rd Street
New York, New York 10022-5299

Copyright © 1993 by Charlie McDade
ISBN: 0-06-100628-9

First HarperTorch paperback printing: October 2003
First HarperPaperbacks printing: November 1993

HarperCollins®, HarperTorch™, and ❦™ are trademarks of HarperCollins Publishers Inc.

Printed in the United States of America

Visit HarperTorch on the World Wide Web at www.harpercollins.com

10 9 8 7 6 5 4 3 2 1

Brady's Law

1

HORSES, GOD LOVE THEM, they were a pain in the butt. Beautiful, graceful, spirited, necessary animals. But a pain in the butt, nonetheless. If Dan Brady had only known how much trouble a few horses could be, he might have thought about some other way to make a living. Lying in the tangled undergrowth at The Wilderness, minié balls clipping the leaves over his head like crazy locusts, he had kept his head down, and on, by planning the rest of his life. It had been crazy to think there would be a rest of his life, but he knew he had to think about anything but the war if he wanted to survive it.

He had seen too many zealots, and too many fools, take the war seriously. He had seen most of them buried, too, and the raw earth looked so much the same waiting for them, he wasn't sure there was a damn bit of difference between the two types. Now, trying to make ends meet and keep a roof over his family's head, he understood what had driven those men. He had been a zealot of another kind, and now he felt like such a fool he knew there was no difference.

And building a corral was no picnic, either. He tossed his hammer onto the stack of raw lumber intended for the fence he wondered if he'd ever finish. Stepping back to measure the distance with his eye, he realized he was less than half finished and had just run out of nails. It was just as well, too, he thought. He was so tired he doubted he could lift the hammer again, let alone drive anything into the stubborn timber. His eyes stung with sweat, and the flies were driving him crazy. Reaching for his canteen, he cursed at its lack of heft, unscrewed the cap, and tilted his head for the last few drops of water. It was now as empty as the nail keg. He threw it onto the boards, and it rattled and bumped all the way down the stack, an old drunk falling downstairs.

"Dan, why don't you take a break, honey? You've been at it all morning."

When he turned, Molly was standing right behind him, her smile a bit strained. He hadn't heard her coming, and her voice had startled him.

"Can't afford to. If I don't get this damn fence built, we'll be chasing horses up and down the valley for a month. It was tough enough rounding them up once. I don't want to do it again."

"You look exhausted."

Brady grunted, then flopped on the ground next to the pile of wood. He looked up at his wife, but with the bright sun behind her and the sweat in his eyes, he could barely see her. He patted the dry grass to his left, but Molly shook her head.

"I can't stay. I just wanted to know when you'd be ready for dinner."

"I'm ready now, I guess. But I'm too damn tired to eat anything. And I have to go into Nogales."

"Whatever for?"

"Need some more nails. Wes Fraser told me I didn't buy enough, but I wouldn't listen. Now I got to make another trip. And listen to him say I told you so without really sayin' it."

"Can't you go tomorrow?"

"Nope, I can't. I can't waste a whole afternoon when I'm not half done with this corral. And I got to work on the barn some, too."

"At least eat something before you go."

Brady didn't say anything. He knew Molly was right, and he was hungry. But there was so much to do, it seemed as if he could work around the clock the rest of his life and still not be finished. He nodded, and she took it, rightly, to mean he would eat before he went into town. He didn't feel like it, and he didn't feel like hitching the team, and most of all he didn't feel like listening to the squeak of the wagon all the way into Nogales and all the way back.

He looked back up at Molly, but she was gone, had left as silently as she had come. He wiped his hands on the seat of his pants as he rose, then checked his palms for new blisters.

Molly was already inside as he crossed the yard, kicking idly at clumps of dusty grass. He couldn't understand how she kept her spirit in so damn dry, and godforsaken, a place. Horses, hell! He'd be better off back East, working for somebody else. At least he wouldn't have to worry about paying his bills. He'd draw a wage, and spend what he made. This was too damn risky. But maybe it would get better when the corral was finished, and he could add to the small spread. Maybe, but he wouldn't count on it.

As it was, he knew Fraser had been right. He shouldn't have planned on nailing the corral together in the first place, but if he was going to do it, he should have listened and bought more nails, like the storekeeper had told him. He had a lot to learn. He was already learning there were better ways of doing things out here than he was used to. But that was cold comfort. He scraped his boots on the rough-bristled brush nailed alongside the sill, and pushed open the door, waving away a few flies that tried to slip in with him.

"Where is everybody today?"

His wife answered without turning, buttering two thick slabs of dark, heavy bread, and carving several thin slices of chicken to finish a sandwich for him. "They went over to the Marshall place. Jenny has a new bunch of puppies. She told the children they could have their pick."

"Just what we need, another mouth to feed."

"Dan, it's not that bad. But if you think so, maybe we don't belong here. Maybe we should go back East."

"That's what I've been thinking."

"Do you want to, I mean really?"

"No."

"Then why should we? We haven't given it a chance here, yet."

"It hasn't given us a chance, you mean, don't you?"

"I guess. But it's not like you to give up so easily."

"Easy? Is that what you think it's been? You think I been playing games out there every day for a month?"

"No, of course not! I mean you're usually so stubborn, I don't understand why you're willing to give up now."

Molly brought the sandwich to the table and poured two glasses of tea before sitting across the table from her husband. He watched her sip her drink and wondered whether he was being fair to her and to their children. He hadn't promised her a paradise, but secretly had hoped New Mexico would be one. Maybe not right off, but with a little help from him. Hell, even Adam and Eve had had to work in their paradise. Why not Dan Brady?

It wasn't possible to hope for that any longer. It was all he could do now to hope they'd get through the next few months. She never complained, and there were times when he knew she wanted to. There even were times when he wanted her to, just so he wouldn't feel alone in his disappointment.

The people of Nogales and the surrounding country had been cautious but friendly. Some of them had even pitched in to help build their cabin. It was nature that was hostile, not the natives. And he wasn't used to that. Arid New Mexico was a lot different from Michigan.

It was beautiful, all right. Even Molly had commented on the color of the mountains off to the northwest, how bright the purples and blues were in the morning, before the sun bleached all color out of the earth. But he hadn't come for scenery, and neither had she. They wanted to build something of their own, together—something to leave the children. But it was tougher going than either of them had expected. He didn't want to quit, but he didn't want to be pig-headed, either. Molly was right, he was usually stubborn, but he wanted to change that, too, when he came out here.

One thing he hadn't shared with her was his intention to make himself over as surely as they hoped to make over their lives. That was his secret, and the thought of letting her in on it only to have to admit failure was more of a risk than he had been willing to take. Better to harbor the secret, keep it close, let her notice it on her own one day, maybe years ahead, sitting on the gallery and watching the sunset.

In the war, he'd learned some things about himself he didn't like. New Mexico was supposed to be new country, and he'd been determined to be a new man. For himself, more than for Molly, though he hoped she'd notice the change and think it an improvement. Looking around the dreary, inhospitable kitchen, Molly was the only thing he saw that he wouldn't trade to be someplace else. And he wondered how long she could remain impervious to the aggressive climate. Her figure was as good as ever, her hair still as black as coal. But he thought he noticed a strand or two of gray. At thirty-one, she was too young, so he didn't ask.

Mornings in front of the shaving mirror, he'd seen changes in himself, too. The smooth pink cheeks, like apples his mother said, had developed a little character, lines that had as much to do with worry as the strong sun of New Mexico, whose bronze had buried the pink. He was still tall, nearly six feet, but his back felt a little tired, as if it wanted to bend under the weight of a heavy burden he couldn't see in the mirror but knew was there all the same. His hair was the same dirty blond, and the scar under his left eye was still there, the same little buttonhook curl. Continuities, he thought, ways for him to recognize himself, just in case there was any doubt. A hundred and eighty pounds of determination, that's how he liked to think of himself. But it was getting harder and harder to keep on thinking like that.

Suddenly, unbearably confined by the barebones kitchen, he pushed back his chair. "I got to go, honey. No sense waiting all day. The work can wait longer than I can."

"When'll you be back, Dan?"

"Soon's I can."

As he crossed to the barn, he examined it, noticing ruefully how the amount of work it needed seemed to grow as he approached. At a distance, it looked rather picturesque, he remembered. Now, he seldom got far enough away to appreciate it. Hitching the team, he bounced out the gate and onto the none-too-parallel stretch of ruts that pretended to be the road to town. The countryside was dry, mocked by the snow on the distant mountains. Almost too white to look at for long in bright sunlight, it was ironic that so much of the water needed to make life more bearable was locked in a beautiful, sterile fastness that would, he knew, lose much of its charm if he drew closer.

Nogales was little more than a collection of boxes, no two the same size or shape. They seemed to have been made from the same shipment of lumber, and certainly had been bleached gray by the same unforgiving sun. The streets were bone dry, the dust so deep each transit left a trace that vanished with the first gust of wind. And that was usually not long in coming, and usually too hot by half when it got there.

Fraser's General Store was a center of activity second only to the Double Eagle Saloon. The only things Wes Fraser didn't sell were whiskey and women, both of which could be had at the Double Eagle, and for about the same price. The latter he knew by rumor only, but didn't doubt it. It was harder to find good whiskey than a woman down on her luck in this part of the country.

Brady pulled his wagon up to the front of the store, locked the brake, and wrapped the reins around it. He stepped down to the rickety wooden walk that joined the strip of commercial buildings, and walked to the back of the buckboard to lower the tailgate. He'd be out with a load in his arms and didn't want to add to the pain in his back by having to pick anything up twice. Before entering the store, he looked up and down the street and didn't see a soul. Apparently he was the only fool willing to brave the heat.

The shade of Fraser's was no cooler than the open air, but at least he was out of the sun. So far out, in fact, that he had to blink twice before he could see anything. Wes Fraser was in the back room, but spotted him as soon as he came in.

"Dan, what brings you down here today? Forget somethin'?"

"Need some more nails," Brady said softly.

"What, nails? Hell, you already bought half a damn keg, just the other day. Didn't lose any on the way home, did you?"

"Nope. Bent a few goin' in, though. What kind of crap you selling these days, Wes?"

"Don't try to skin me, Dan. I told you you'd need more'n you bought."

"What can I say, Wes? You were right."

The merchant laughed and wiped his hands on his apron, showering his feet with fine flour dust from the sacks he had been stacking in the storeroom. "What can I sell you today, Mr. Brady?"

"More nails and some wood softener, if you got any."

"Wish to hell I did, Dan," he said, laughing again. "I could sell more'n I could stock, for damn sure."

"I reckon you would."

"How many nails you want?"

"You tell me."

"I think another half-keg ought to do, 'less you plan on going right to work on that barn."

"Not in this life, Wes. I do need some other things, though," Brady said, pulling a list from his jeans.

"Why don't you just give that list here, and I'll fix you right up."

As he reached for the paper, a shaft of sun flashed across the counter, and Brady turned to see three cowboys entering the store, horsing around and shoving one another through the narrow entrance.

2

"HEY THERE, MR. FRASER," the tallest of the three said, more loudly than necessary. "How you doing?"

"Cody, I'm fine. How are you?"

"All right, all right, there, Wesley. All right."

"You boys know Dan Brady?" Fraser asked.

"Nope," Cody said, turning to Dan. "I don't."

"Dan, this here's Cody Fallon, and them other two boys are Jim Anderson and Don Gallup. Don's the ugly one."

Dan smiled and reached out to shake Fallon's hand, then stepped to one side to do the same with Anderson and Gallup. It was obvious from Fallon's breath he had been drinking. So had the others. Anderson shook perfunctorily, but Gallup ignored Brady's offered hand. "Nice to meet you," Dan said, not certain he meant it.

"I'll be with you boys in just a minute," Fraser said, looking at Dan's list again.

"Don't feel like waiting, Wes," Gallup said. His voice was husky and whiskey slurred. "Specially for a stranger."

"Well, now, Don, you'll just have to. Dan was here first, and he ain't no stranger."

"Is to me, Wes."

"But it's my store, Don."

"Horseshit!"

"Come on, Don, wait your turn." Fallon laughed. "We ain't in a big hurry anyhow."

Gallup walked to the end of the counter and hoisted himself up, his spurs rattling against its front. "Ain't got all day," he mumbled.

"Don's right," Anderson chimed in. "Hell, Wes, we just need a couple things. Why don't you give 'em to us, and we'll get out of your hair."

"Like I said, boys," Fraser answered, "Dan was here first. Cody, why don't you talk some sense into these boys later, or leave them home next time."

Fallon looked uncomfortable. Whether he was the soberest of the three, or the most polite, Dan didn't know. He was anxious to be on his way, and tapped his fingers nervously on the counter while Fraser rounded up the items on Brady's list.

"Hell, let's get out of here, Jimmy," Gallup said, jumping down from his perch. "Cody wants to wait, let him. I'm leaving."

He walked to the door and turned to wait for Anderson, who looked uncertainly at Fallon before following Gallup outside. Fallon seemed embarrassed and smiled wanly at Brady. "We had a few drinks before we come over here," he said.

"That would've been my guess," Brady said.

"We ain't drunk, though," Fallon said. "Just a little rowdy."

"No kidding?" Brady didn't want to ignore the man, but he didn't feel much like talking to him, either. The mood he was in, he was likely to say something he'd regret.

He watched Fraser pick the last couple of items from a shelf and place them in a neat stack on the end of the counter. "You want this on account, Dan, or cash and carry?"

"On account, I guess, Wes. Thanks."

"On account of what?" Fallon asked. Dan turned to look at him sharply. "Just joking, Brady," he said. "Nice to meet you."

Brady nodded and grabbed the first package and lugged it out to the wagon. As he turned to go back in, Fallon was in the doorway with a sack over each shoulder, one of flour and one of beans. The big cowboy stepped lightly onto the boardwalk and leaned over the side of the wagon to place them carefully on the wagon bed. "I'm obliged, Mr. Fallon," Dan said, trying to hide his surprise.

Fallon walked back into the store, Dan following to get the half-keg of nails. Dan lifted the heavy container and waddled outside, placing the keg on the tailgate with a thud, then climbed up to wheel it on its rim back into the wagon.

Dropping to the ground, Brady listened to the voices, quite angry now, almost unintelligible. Fraser was shouting to the men to get out of his store. He walked back onto the boardwalk and stuck his head into the gloomy interior of the store. Wes was shaking his head. "I told you, no, dammit, no credit. Now git."

"Anything wrong, Wes?" Brady asked.

Don Gallup whirled, nearly losing his balance. "Ain't none of your business if there's something wrong, or not," he barked. "Why don't you just git on home to the little woman, and keep your nose out of where it don't belong?"

"Nothing I can't handle, Dan," Fraser said. "Thanks."

Brady nodded. He paused to look at Fallon, who seemed embarrassed somehow, scraping the toe of one boot on the scarred wooden floor, then bending to pick up whatever it was he'd kicked loose. The cowboy looked at him then, tossed whatever it was over the counter into a barrel Fraser used for trash, and shrugged, as if to say, *I don't know what to do about him, but he's a friend.*

Gallup, delighted to have yet another focus for

his anger, took a couple of steps toward Brady, his fists balling and unclenching as if he were having some sort of seizure. "Told you this weren't none of your affair, farmboy. . . ." His face, despite the sunburn, seemed to pinken, starting at his chin and rising like the mercury in a thermometer. "You hear?"

Dan stepped into the store then. He wasn't looking for a fight, but he knew enough about Gallup and men like him to know that the surest way to bring on a fight was to run from one. At the moment, Gallup had the look of a man who wasn't going to be satisfied until he bloodied somebody's nose. Brady was conscious of the gun on Gallup's hip and felt more than a little vulnerable. He almost never wore a sidearm, and his carbine was out in the wagon. He was starting to wish he'd listened to Wes Fraser the last time. If he'd bought enough nails on the first trip, he thought, he wouldn't be there now.

But wishing wouldn't get it done, and Gallup seemed determined now to drag Brady into his own private rage. Brady felt the tug of it, like a man on the edge of a tornado, watching the howling winds spiral toward him, feeling their pull, knowing that any second he would get sucked in and, unless he were luckier than he had a right to be, torn apart by something he didn't understand and couldn't control.

Fallon seemed like the best avenue, and Brady nodded to him. "Mr. Fallon, maybe you ought to take your friends down the street for a cup of coffee. No sense in letting things get ugly. Gallup, here, 'll end up doing something he regrets."

Fallon seemed uncertain how to proceed, and he tucked his hands into his belt while he chewed on his lower lip. But Gallup was not about to let Cody Fallon, or anybody else, tell him what to do. Not at the moment, anyway. He took three quick steps toward Brady, lost his footing, and Brady had to reach out to catch him to keep him from falling on his face.

Fallon shook his head, his expression a mixture of good humor and embarrassment. He hoisted himself up on the counter and sat there, his crossed legs thumping against the counter's front like it was a drum.

As he tried to get Gallup upright, the smell of whiskey swirled around him, and Brady turned his head to avoid the sour stink of it. That was his mistake. Gallup, seeing an opening, brought a roundhouse up off the floor, and caught Brady on the side of the head, knocking his hat off. The blow was a glancing one, but it stunned Brady for a second. He couldn't believe it had happened, and it was the surprise as much as the punch itself that seemed to freeze him in his tracks.

Gallup, thinking he had a clear shot, ducked

into a crouch and took a step closer. He cocked his right arm, thinking to get in another roundhouse. Brady, though, saw it coming, caught the punch, and twisted Gallup's arm, spinning the drunken cowboy around and tugging the arm up in a hammerlock.

Brady shoved Gallup, forcing him to move closer to the counter. Fallon slid to the floor, and when he reached out, Brady let his prisoner go. Fallon grabbed Gallup as he spun around. Gallup stood there tottering from side to side, his bleary eyes swimming in and out of focus.

"You best go on, Mr. Brady," Fallon said. "I think I can handle him now."

Brady looked at Wes Fraser, who had his arms folded across his chest, resting on the rounded ledge of his belly just above the top of his apron. "It's all right, Dan. There won't be no trouble. You go on and tend to your shopping. You expect to get that fence up, you can't be riding herd on drunken cowboys all day long."

Brady waited for Gallup to say something, but the cowboy just glared, his jaw tight, knots of muscle writhing like cats in a burlap bag just under the skin.

Fraser waved to him with a shooing motion, as if Brady were some stray cat he wanted out of his garden.

Fallon flashed him a grin. "Me and Mr. Fraser can hold the fort," he said.

Brady wasn't quite so sure as Fallon seemed to be, but he turned and headed for the front door, feeling a tightness in his shoulders. He still had a few things to pick up, and when he stepped out into the sun, he stretched, trying to release the tension in his back and neck. Puffing out his cheeks, he stepped into the street and started toward the dry-goods store. Molly needed some cloth, and he remembered the swatch she'd tucked into his pocket, fished it out, and twisted it around one finger as he walked.

Hardy Mumms had a mouth full of straight pins when Dan walked in. Mabel Mumms stood wrapped like a mummy in the brightest cloth Brady had ever seen. Hardy looked more than a little flustered. He nodded, and tried to speak, scattering the pins in a shiny cascade that rattled faintly on the floor.

"Hardy, darn it all, see what you done?" Mabel started to spin like a top, tearing the cloth from her shoulders and chest, scolding him the whole time, her words rising and falling as she faced her husband, then away. She was trying to adjust her volume to compensate for her rotation, but her timing was off. When she had extricated herself from the bright red-and-blue cotton, she put her hands on her hips. "I swear, you're as useless as an umbrella in a hurricane."

Hardy looked at Brady, but his words were directed toward Mabel. "Told you I wasn't no good at tailoring. Reason I sell cloth is it's the only thing I know how to do with it. Let me tend to business, Mabel, and we'll see can we get it right after lunch."

Mabel smiled at Brady. "Dan, you as helpless as this old lump of mine, are you?"

Brady laughed. He untangled the cloth from his finger, and said, "All I'm fit for is to fetch the stuff home, Mabel."

"Molly has my sympathy," Mabel said. "Men," she grunted, "as worthless by the bushel as the peck." She snatched the sample from Brady's hand. "How much you need?"

"Four yards, if you have it."

"I'm sure we do. Hardy, get them shears out of your pocket and give me a hand." She walked to a long table where bolts of cloth were stacked like cords of firewood, rummaged in a pile predominantly blue, the sample in one hand, until she found the match. She unrolled the cloth by giving the bolt a shove and jerking the loose end in the opposite direction, then took a yardstick. Hardy happened to be approaching at the time, and the way he flinched, Brady guessed the merchant had seen the yardstick put to less peaceful use than measuring cloth.

But he braved the storm, made an even cut just ahead of Mabel's indicative fingertip, and tucked the shears back into his pocket. "Anything else I can get you, Dan?"

Brady shook his head. "Not today, thanks, Hardy." Mabel folded the cloth, wrapped it in paper, and tied it with string. When she thrust it at him, she smiled, but the package nearly knocked the breath from his lungs, and he guessed that Hardy was in deep water for the rest of the afternoon. "How much do I owe you?"

"Eighty-eight cents. I'll just put it on your account."

"Molly's account," Mabel corrected, and neither man dared argue.

"Thanks, Hardy, Mabel . . ." Brady touched his hat brim, and turned to leave.

Behind him, Mabel shouted, "You say hello home, Daniel Brady." He nodded and ducked outside again, breathing a sigh of relief. He walked back to his wagon, glancing at the front of Wes Fraser's store as he slipped the cloth in among the other packages, then climbed over the tailgate and forward to the seat.

As he checked one final time that the supplies were secure for the trip home, he heard glass shatter—by the sound of it, somewhere behind the store or the next-door barbershop. When he stepped down from the wagon, he heard shouting. One of the voices was Wes Fraser's. He paused, debating whether to go back in, then decided Wes could take care of himself. He'd likely just make things worse if he went back. And he wasn't even sure it came from the store.

Besides, he thought, Fallon didn't seem any more than a bit high-spirited, and Fraser hadn't indicated dislike of the man. For all Dan knew, they always did business in this unusual manner.

As Brady unraveled the reins, there was a loud report—a gunshot, from the sound of it. This time he was sure it had come from the store.

3

BRADY JUMPED OUT OF THE WAGON, in his haste forgetting the Winchester carbine under the seat. He reached back into the wagon, grabbed the carbine, and started for the door of Fraser's store. As he stepped onto the wooden walkway, he heard glass breaking somewhere inside, and stopped in his tracks. He ducked into a crouch, and steeled himself for a rush toward the door from the men inside.

When nothing happened, he crept close to the open door and called, "Wes? Wes Fraser, you all right?"

There was no answer. Brady looked down the street and saw that people were going about their business as usual, apparently unaware of the commotion inside the store.

Once more, he leaned forward. "Wes, it's Dan Brady, you all right?"

Again, the store was quiet. He tried to peer into the gloom, but the bright sun outside made the doorway an opaque wall beyond which he could see nothing but piled gray and black shadows. It was the silence, though, that frightened him. Gallup and the others hadn't come out, and standing in the doorway would make him a perfect target. He needed help, and there was no one close enough.

Backing away from the doorway, Brady jumped off the boardwalk and ducked low as he slipped in behind the wagon. Keeping the wagon bed between himself and the doorway, he eased forward, toward his team, keeping his eyes fixed on the black rectangle that still seemed to promise an eruption of boots and chaps.

He could see Al Fisher, his white smock gray behind the dirty window of his barbershop, bent over his chair. "Al," he shouted, "Al Fisher."

The barber stopped, his clippers at half-mast, and looked around. His lips moved, as if he was asking the man in the chair whether he'd heard anything. The customer turned toward the glass, and Brady waved frantically. The man sat up, and Fisher turned toward the window. As the customer jumped to his feet, Fisher ran to the door of his shop and poked his head out.

"What's going on, Dan?" he hollered, when he spotted Brady's waving arms.

"Not sure. I heard a gunshot in Wes Fraser's. I called but nobody answers. Keep an eye on the store, will you? I'm going to get the sheriff."

The customer, still wearing the barber cloak clotted with locks of salt and pepper, stepped outside. Brady knew him. It was Clayton Riddle, the owner of one of the largest spreads in the Nogales valley.

Riddle started to walk toward him. Then, suddenly conscious of the cloak, he brushed at it, trying to rid it of the clumps of hair as if they were bugs. Finally he tore it from around his neck, balled it up, shoved it at Fisher, and stepped into the street.

"Dan," he said, "I'll keep an eye out here. You go on and get Matt Lowry."

Riddle ducked under the bobbing heads of Brady's team and moved in behind the wagon, his gun drawn.

Fisher was still standing there, the clippers in one hand, the balled cloak clutched against his stomach by the other. Brady started to run. It was two blocks to Lowry's office, and as he raced up the street, the Winchester still in his hand, he saw people stop what they were doing. Suddenly lined with statues, the main street of Nogales took on the air of a museum.

Somebody called to him as he raced past, but Brady couldn't hear what was said, and he turned and waved toward the store. He saw a couple of cowboys take a step or two, then stop, confused and uncertain.

When he reached the sheriff's office, Lowry was just getting up from his battered desk, holding a hammer and a sheet of paper. Several tacks jutted from between his lips like shiny snaggleteeth.

Lowry grabbed the paper with his hammer hand, spat the tacks into his empty palm, and said, "The hell's the matter, Dan? You look like you seen a ghost."

"Been a shooting, down to Wes Fraser's."

"What? A shooting? Who?"

Brady shook his head. "I don't know. I heard a shot. I called to Wes but he didn't answer."

Lowry tossed the hammer, paper, and tacks onto the desk, and moved out from behind it with a single long stride. Already, the flush on his normally ruddy cheeks had deepened and begun to spread. His white mustache bobbed, and he stroked it with chubby fingers as he clapped his hat on, spraying wisps of white out from under the brim.

"Let's go have a look," he said.

Brady waited for Lowry to lead the way out into the heat.

The sheriff waddled a bit, his short legs pumping like crazy pistons, and he turned to make sure that Dan was behind him. When they reached Brady's wagon, Al Fisher and Clay Riddle were crouched behind it, the barber still armed only with his scissors.

"Matt," Riddle said. "How do?"

"Anything happening in there?" Lowry asked, after nodding hello.

Fisher just clicked his shears and bobbed his head in greeting.

"You fixin' to cut somebody up with them things, Al?" the sheriff asked.

Fisher looked at the scissors as if he'd never seen them before, then tucked them into the breast pocket of his smock.

Riddle chuckled, then shook his head. "Ain't seen nothing moving. Ain't heard a sound. I called to Wes a time or two, but there wasn't no answer."

Lowry turned to Brady. "Dan, you sure what you heard was a gunshot?"

Brady nodded. "No doubt in my mind, Sheriff. I was in the store just before I heard it. Wes was having a bit of an argument with some cowboys. Said he could handle it, and I went on over to Hardy Mumms's place. Then I came back to the wagon. I was fixin' to go when I heard it."

"Who were the drovers? You know 'em?"

"Wes introduced us. Fella named Cody Fallon was there, and two others, Don Gallup and Anderson, somebody Anderson."

"Jim Anderson?" Riddle asked.

"That's it."

"Them are three of your boys, ain't they Clay?" Lowry asked.

"Yeah, they are. A little rough around the edges, but they ain't given to shootin' up storekeepers. Not as far as I know, anyhow."

"Well," Lowry said, drawing his pistol, "no sense in staying out here all afternoon. Might as well see what's what. Clay, how about you and Al go on around back, in case anybody comes out the back way. Me and Dan will go in the front."

"Sure thing." The rancher looked at Fisher for a moment. "Al, you got anything but them shears?"

"Got a shotgun in the shop. Ain't but loaded with birdshot."

"Go on and git it."

Fisher swallowed hard, then patted his pocket as if to make sure he still had the clippers. He ducked low and dashed toward the boardwalk in front of his shop, and Riddle followed him. The barber disappeared into his shop for a moment, and when he came out, he was holding a rather ancient looking Remington, and he had taken off his smock. To get around behind Fraser's, the two men had to use an alley alongside the barbershop, and as they disappeared, Lowry yelled, "I'll count to twenty, 'fore I do anything, Clay."

Riddle yelled something unintelligible, but Lowry took it as acknowledgement. "One . . . two . . . three . . ."

On twenty, Lowry licked his lips. "Guess it's time, Dan," he said, as he ducked out from behind the wagon and sprinted for the boardwalk.

His boots thumped on the hollow planking, and when he reached the wall of the store, he squatted down right beside the door, then waved for Brady to join him.

Dan kept his eye on the open door, dashed to the storefront, and knelt down behind the sheriff. Sensing Brady behind him, he leaned forward and called, "Wes, this is Matt Lowry. You all right in there?"

There was no answer.

Lowry changed tack. "Listen to me . . . anybody in there, this is the sheriff. I'm comin' in. You know what's good for you, you'll lay down your guns before I come. Anybody with a gun in his hand will be fair game."

The empty doorway swallowed the words the way a dry well swallows a leaf. There was not even a whisper. Brady moved onto Lowry's hip. "I'll nip across to the other side, Matt," he said. "I can cover you better from there."

Lowry glanced at Brady and winked agreement. Brady straightened and leaped across the opening, half expecting to hear a gunshot, and knowing that if he did, the bullet would already have hit him or missed before he knew it had been fired. But the only sound was the thump of his heels on the weathered planks.

"Enough of this horseshit!" Lowry muttered. "I'm going in." He adjusted his grip on the Colt Peacemaker in his hand and dove through the opening, landing with a thump that expelled the air from his lungs in a tortured grunt.

Brady followed him in, taking cover behind a mound of shadows that, up close, resolved themselves into a stack of feed sacks. The musty stink of the grain tickled his nostrils, and he suppressed a sneeze with his free hand. He pressed his cheek against the rough cloth, reached up to take off his hat, and set it on the floor behind him.

"Wes," Brady called, "Wes?"

This time, he heard a groan.

"You hear that, Matt?" he whispered.

"I heard it . . . Wes?"

This time there was no answering groan, and Lowry expelled his breath in exasperation. He gave Brady a hand signal to tell him he was going to the far wall, then work his way toward the counter.

As he started to move, Clay Riddle called from out back.

"Sheriff, the window's busted out back here. You see anything?"

Before he could answer, another groan seeped out of the shadows, and Brady started to creep around the feed sacks, his boots scraping on the rough floorboards. The Winchester was unwieldy, hardly ideal for quick movement in close quarters, but it was all he had, and he kept it in front of him, stock between his legs as he duck-walked down a narrow aisle between the sacks and a long wooden table.

Off to his left, a blade of light speared in through a high window. Dust motes swarmed like gnats, and a single fly darted into the light with an angry snarl before landing out of sight.

Something moved, and Brady thumbed back the hammer on the Winchester. He saw a shadow behind the counter and started to bring the rifle up, but Clay Riddle hissed, "It's Clay, Sheriff, don't shoot. There ain't nobody back here."

"Find a lamp or something, would you, Clay?" Lowry called, his voice echoing in the high-ceilinged room.

"Hold on, here's Wes. Christ, he's bleeding like a stuck pig."

Brady got to his feet and ran toward the counter. On the way, he tripped over something jutting out from behind a row of barrels, stumbled, and landed hard on both knees. He turned to see what had tripped him. It was a booted foot. "Somebody here?" he called.

Leaning over the prostrate form, he could just make out the man's features in the shadows. "It's Cody Fallon," he said.

4

"AL, GET YOUR ASS IN HERE," Lowry barked. He moved the lamp close to the edge of the counter and turned the wick up. In the pale wash of orange, the ugly stain on the front of Wes Fraser's apron looked brown with gold flecks. "Jesus," Lowry said, "he's hurt bad."

Looking up at Fisher, the sheriff dispatched him for help. "Get a couple of boys over here, buttonhole the first men you see, then go on and tell Doc Mitchell we're comin'."

Fisher backed away, never quite taking his eyes off the man on the floor, but never quite looking directly at him, either.

"What's the story with Fallon, Clay?" Lowry asked.

"Got a bump on his head, but he don't look shot. Must have hit his head on something, I reckon."

"All three of them were pretty drunk," Brady said. "Fallon seemed all right, but the others were kind of nasty."

"They're good boys, all three of 'em," Riddle said. "Like anybody, they get a few drinks under their belts, they like to cut up some, but this"—he shook his head—"this ain't like them. I don't know what the hell happened here."

Riddle straightened, grabbed a spare apron from the counter, and went outside. "Gonna get some water," he said.

Lowry was busy cutting away the bloodstained apron from Wes Fraser's motionless form. The shirt underneath was slippery and slick with blood, and Brady could see an ugly tear in the cloth and, beneath it, an uglier hole just above the merchant's left hip and toward his middle, about halfway between the hip and belt buckle.

Fraser moaned once or twice, but he was in a bad way. His eyes never flickered, and the moans were nothing more than that, no attempt to speak. "This don't look good at all, Dan," Lowry said.

Before Brady could say anything, Clay Riddle was back, a sopping apron balled in one fist. He walked to the aisle where Fallon still lay unconscious and squeezed the apron tight enough to send a rush of water over the cowboy's face and head. Brady could see a thick welt, three inches or so long, over Fallon's left eye, disappearing up around the hairline. It was an angry red and was already beginning to turn purple.

"Must have hit his head or something," Riddle said. "Probably too damn drunk to stand up."

Two men rushed into the store and stopped when they saw Brady and Riddle. "Sheriff here?" the taller of the two asked.

Brady knew him by sight but not by name. The other one he'd never seen before.

"Over here," Lowry called, and the two men moved down the aisle and past Brady. The tall man glanced down at Fallon as he moved by. "What the hell happened to Cody?" he asked.

He looked at Brady as if expecting him to answer. Brady shook his head. "Don't know," he said.

"Quit your jawin' and gimme a hand with Wes," Lowry snapped.

The two men moved in behind the counter. The shorter of the two turned away. "Jesus Christ, what happened to him?" he asked, trying hard to keep his lunch down.

"Somebody shot him, you horse's ass. What's it look like happened? Grab a hold. We're gonna take him to Doc Mitchell's."

"Maybe we ought to let the doc look at him before we move him, Matt," Riddle suggested.

"No time. He's sinkin' fast, Clay. Doc'll just come in, look at him, and tell us to take Wes over to his office." The sheriff continued pressing the bloody apron against the wound as he scrunched over to let the two newcomers in behind the counter. "Grab him under the shoulders, Jake. Let Diego take his feet, and I'll keep the pressure on. It's a long walk to Doc's office."

"Put him in my wagon, Sheriff," Brady said. He moved toward the front door without waiting for an argument. Behind the wagon, he lowered the tailgate and climbed in to shift some of the supplies until there was enough room for Fraser to lie on the wagon bed. By the time he was finished, the three bearers were already on the boardwalk. Jake and Diego staggered toward the edge of the wooden walk and down into the street. Lowry stayed between them and leaned toward Fraser's bowed body, one stiffened forearm pressing the bloody cloth against the wound.

Lowry climbed into the wagon bed and waited for Jake to close the tailgate. "Jake," he said, "you and Diego stay here with Clay. Tell him I don't want Fallon goin' nowhere till I get a chance to talk to him."

"Cody done it?" Jake asked.

"Hell, I don't know. Don't nobody know for sure but Wes and the shooter, but Fallon's the only one in the store, and I got to believe that if he didn't do it, he knows who did."

Brady was already on the wagon seat, the reins

in his hand. He was waiting for Lowry to give him the order to move, which Lowry must have sensed, because the sheriff turned and tilted his head back. "Let's git, Dan."

The wagon lurched as Brady clucked to the team and jerked the reins.

Lowry was perched on his heels and nearly lost his balance. He had to let go of the compression bandage to grab the side of the wagon, and cursed under his breath.

Brady saw Doc Mitchell hurrying toward him down the center of the street, now lined with curious onlookers as the word had spread. People were standing in doorways, and a few even hung out of second-story windows watching the wagon and its peculiar cargo.

Mitchell waved, then turned and hurried back the way he'd come. When the wagon covered the two blocks to his office, he was standing on the landing, his black bag dangling from one clenched fist.

As Brady set the brake, Mitchell scurried up the remaining stairs and opened his office door. Lowry impressed a couple of the curious to help carry the wounded man up the steps. Brady and Lowry took Fraser under the arms while the other two men took his legs.

Mitchell had already lit a lamp and was taking off his coat when the patient was carried in. "Put him on the table, boys," he said.

When Fraser had been laid on the padded table, Lowry chased the two men outside and closed the door.

Mitchell walked to the table to get a closer look. "Jesus," he said, "that don't look good at all."

"You're the doctor. You ain't supposed to talk like that," Lowry reminded him.

"Hell yes, I'm the doctor, but facts are facts, and this particular fact is that Wes don't have but a fifty-fifty chance, and that's if he's lucky." He used a scalpel to slice through the matted cloth of Fraser's shirt, cut the apron strings, and unbuckled the merchant's belt.

He grunted as he lifted Fraser's hip and looked at the exit wound in the back. "Looks to me like the bullet prob'ly went through his liver and a kidney." Mitchell shook his head, smacking his lips in disapproval. "Umnh, umnh, umnh . . . that is plain ugly, Matt."

"Do what you can. I got to get back to the store and see what's what."

"Anybody gone to tell Sarah what happened?"

"You know how this town is, Doc," Lowry answered. "More than likely there was a foot race. Seems like bad news needs half a dozen messengers. If it's real bad, they get in a fist fight on the way, vyin' for the privilege of tellin' it."

"Then I reckon there was a regular Donnybrook on the way out to Fraser's place."

Lowry touched Brady on the shoulder. "Come on, Dan, let's go talk to Cody Fallon, if he's awake. And if he ain't, I plan to kick him until he is."

"Cody Fallon done this?" Mitchell asked.

"That's the way it looks."

"What on earth for? That don't seem like Cody."

"Hell, you get a man full of whiskey, not much of anything he does seems like him. That goes for Cody Fallon, too, I reckon."

Lowry led the way, pausing at the door just long enough to say, "I'll stop by in a bit, Doc. There's any news, you see to it I hear about it, will you?"

"Sure thing."

"First, I mean."

"I know that. You'll be the first, but I don't expect we'll know anything for a few hours. If Wes makes it through the night, he's got a chance. But . . ." Mitchell didn't finish, because he didn't have to. Lowry knew very well what the alternative was.

On the way back to Fraser's store, the sheriff took his time, stopping at the foot of the stairs to roll a cigarette. "You say you didn't actually see nothing, that right, Dan?"

Brady nodded. "That's right. I saw Fallon, Gallup, and Anderson in the store. There was an argument of some kind, not sure what about. I stuck my head in, had a little set to with Gallup, but that was all. Wes seemed like he wasn't worried, so I went on to Hardy's place. When I got back to the wagon, I heard a commotion, what sounded like glass breaking. And the gunshot."

"And you say nobody come out of the store, that right?"

"Right. Not the front door, anyway. And I didn't go in, because I figured all three of them were still in there. I called to Wes, but he didn't answer. Neither did anybody else. That's when I went for you. Clay Riddle and Al Fisher watched the front."

"They didn't see nothing either, then, I guess."

Brady shook his head. "Clay was in the barber chair when the gun went off. I don't know what they saw, if anything, while I was down this way. You'll have to ask them about that."

"Don't think I won't, Dan. I don't like this. Not one damn bit. I know Cody Fallon's a nice young fellow and all, but I won't stand for nothing like this. Innocent folks got a right to be left alone. What it is, you ask me, it's that damn whiskey. I had my way, Nogales'd be dry as a bone."

Brady grunted. "We better get on down to the store, Matt."

Reluctantly, Lowry agreed, but Brady noticed that he didn't seem in a big hurry. There was a small crowd around the front of the store, mostly cowboys, and a few aproned merchants. They were standing in small knots, talking among themselves.

"How's Wes, Sheriff?" Donald Carter, who ran

the bank and doubled as mayor, asked. "He gonna pull through?"

"Have to ask Doc Mitchell about that, Mr. Carter," Lowry said.

"Who done it?"

"Well, now, Mr. Mayor, that's what I got to find out, ain't it?"

"I hear you got the man inside already."

"That right? That's news to me. Right now, all I got is a drunken cowboy with a knot in his head a blind man could see. Whether he shot Wes or not, I don't know."

Lowry started to climb onto the boardwalk, but the mayor wasn't finished. He grabbed Lowry's arm. "Well you better . . ."

Lowry spun around, one foot on the walk and one on the ground. He looked at the fingers gripping his wrist. "No, you'd better, Mr. Carter. You'd better let go of my arm."

Carter glared at him, but he let go, and Lowry went on into the store, Brady right behind him.

Fallon was conscious now, sitting on the counter with his face in his hands. He looked up as Lowry and Brady approached, but said nothing.

"Cody, what happened here?" Lowry asked.

Fallon shook his head. "I don't know, Sheriff. I didn't see nothing."

"And you didn't do nothing, either, I suppose. That right?"

Fallon nodded. "Course I didn't do nothing."

"How'd you get that knot on your head? Low flying bird done it?"

Fallon raised one hand to his temple, and his fingers gingerly traced the three-inch-long welt over his eye. He winced, looked at the trickle of blood on his fingertips, then at Lowry.

"No, it weren't no bird. I don't know what done it."

"You shoot Wes Fraser, did you?"

"No sir, I didn't."

"Who shot him, then? Was it Apaches come in here when we wasn't looking?"

"Sheriff, I told you, I don't know what happened."

Lowry sucked on a tooth, shook his head almost imperceptibly, then sat on the counter alongside Fallon. When he spoke again, he was looking at the floor. "Well, now, Cody, seems like we got us a problem. See Dan Brady here? Well, he seen you and Donny Gallup and Jim Anderson arguing with Wes. Then somebody shoots Wes, and when I come inside, you're the only one here besides Wes himself. Now, what do you think that looks like to me?"

"I told you I didn't do nothing, Sheriff."

Lowry leaned close, took a deep breath, and said, "You been drinking pretty hard, haven't you Cody?"

Fallon didn't answer, but Lowry didn't really seem to expect him to. "Man does a lot of things he shouldn't when he gets to drinkin'. That what happened here, Cody?"

"I already told you, I don't . . ."

"I know what you told me, Cody, but I also know Wes Fraser is up the street with his life hangin' by a thread. He don't make it, I won't be able to ask him what happened. You're the only other one I know for sure I can ask. If Gallup or Anderson were here when the shooting started, why of course I could ask them. Were they here?"

"I don't know."

Lowry shrugged his shoulders, whether in helplessness or exasperation, Brady wasn't sure. "Then I reckon I got no choice but to lock you up, Cody, and see what develops."

Clay Riddle said, "Hang on a minute, Matt. You know me. I'll vouch for the boy. No need to lock him up."

Lowry shook his head. "Can't do that, Clay. The way it is, I got Cody now. I let him go home with you, I might not have him when I need him."

"What about bail?"

"It ain't up to me to decide that, Clay. I'll send for a judge, but it'll take a couple of days." He slipped off the counter, landed with a thud, and took Fallon by the arm. "Come on, Cody. Got to do this as much for your own good as anything. Folks like Wes Fraser a whole lot. Wouldn't want nobody to decide to make this any messier than it is already."

5

THE SUN WAS SETTING by the time Dan Brady got his wagon rolling. The team was frisky, having spent longer than they were used to in the traces, and Brady had to keep a tight rein. As the sky turned purple, great masses of clouds over the mountains were fringed with orange, lacy filigrees trailing away from the huge dark masses that seemed to boil as if they were inhabited by dragons. Now and then, as if to confirm that impression, flaming tongues licked out at the horizon or slavered along the upper edges, and golden blades lanced off in every direction.

He knew he was going to have to tell Molly what had happened to Wes Fraser, and he knew, too, that Molly was going to be upset, maybe even angry. They had come West, she would say, to lead a quiet life, raise the children, and be left alone.

The not-so-hidden meaning of her words would be the same as it always was: she hadn't wanted to come West in the first place. It had been his idea, and it had seemed like a good one, so good, in fact, that he had done what he seldom did—he'd argued with her until she'd given in.

Ohio was more to Molly's liking—peaceful farms, settled neighbors, picket fences, and leaves collecting against the steps every October. But farming, even in Ohio, was a hard way to go, and not much to Dan Brady's taste. He didn't know why, not for sure, although he suspected it had something to do with his father and his grandfather, both of whom had broken their backs on nearly barren Irish land. That was farming at its worst, spending less time planting than digging rocks out of the unforgiving soil, soil that didn't even belong to the men who worked it, trying to subdue it by the strength of will that was their only weapon and their only ally.

Born in New York, in slums that reeked of sewage and teemed with desperate men whose hearts were as black as the steerage holds in which they'd crossed the Atlantic, Brady had grown up tough, tougher than he cared to be, and there were times, still, when he wondered whether that toughness was keeping more than the world at bay. When his father, who had worked on the docks twelve and fourteen hours a day in summer, shorter hours in winter, when the work day began and ended with the sunlight, had managed to scrape together enough money to get his family and his few meager belongings across the Appalachians, Dan had thought things would get better.

But they didn't.

Patrick Brady bought a patch of land that looked like paradise to him, where tall trees, hundreds of years old, their trunks bigger than two men could encircle with their arms, towered over the thick-chested Irishman. It was hard work clearing the land, and there seemed to be a stone for every leaf on every tree under the moss and carpet of rotting leaves. But Patrick was in ecstasy. It was his land, and he had two boys with strong backs to help him till it. And three girls to help their mother carry her end of the bargain. But ecstasy had faded with the summer, and by November, Patrick was bedridden, as if his body had worn itself out looking for a place to die and, having found it, wanted nothing more than to lie down one last time.

He died in early December, and before the New Year, Mary McConnell Brady followed him to the grave. Dan was the oldest, and, at sixteen, he wasn't nearly old enough, but he did what he could. For three years, Dan carried the family on his back, hacking a meager living from the sour earth of Pat Brady's folly.

And then the war came.

At twenty, Dan was the prematurely aging patriarch of a clutch of Irish orphans, but Paddy was just a year younger, and old enough to see to the farm, such as it was, while Dan joined the 18th Ohio Infantry Regiment. When he donned the brand new blue uniform in Columbus on May 7, 1861, he looked down at the clean, bright cloth and realized it was the first time in seven years he had a new pair of pants. It pained him some to leave Paddy, Kathleen, Colleen, and Pegeen behind, but not much. And if slogging through mud with a pack on his back was the price he had to pay, at least the only other weight he had to bear was that of his own flesh and bone. No longer buried under the weight of the family, he'd felt then as if he'd been given a reprieve from a hanging.

He hated himself now for feeling that relief, as much as he understood it, no matter that he could tell himself that it was natural for a young man who'd barely had time to be a boy. The infantry brought freedom of a kind he'd never known, even with the jackasses giving orders and the stink of the camps.

But he paid a price for that freedom. When the war was over and he came home, his sisters were long gone. They'd buried Paddy under the same solitary oak where Dan had buried his mother and

his father. He didn't know until a year later that
the girls had been told he was killed at The Wilderness, and by then it was too late. They had scattered to the winds, leaving no trace, and he didn't
blame them. In a way, he even envied them. They
must have felt the same sense of freedom, of relief,
of a burden lifted, that he had felt marching out of
Columbus.

Molly didn't know much of that, because he
hadn't told her. It pained him to talk about it, and
she often said that he must have been born fully
grown, summoned by the sounds of the cannon at
Fort Sumter. But she knew better than to pry. Even
during their courtship, when he would spend long
hours on the porch swing at her family's home, he
had skirted the issue, revealing just enough to let
her know he did not want to discuss it. He had
been like a man with a price on his head, trying
desperately to cover his tracks and, if he could,
even to erase his own shadow.

It was that sense of the past, the history that
hung like a ghost in the air of the Ohio River valley that had convinced him he had to move West.
Molly had resisted at first, but three years after
their marriage, with Brian already a toddler and
her mother newly buried, she had consented,
knowing that Dan would not give up trying to con-
vince her.

Now Dan was wondering how he could possibly explain to her that things were going to get complicated for a while, complicated in a way they had never been. She was strong, and she loved him almost as much, he thought, as he loved her. And they would manage somehow to get through.

Or so he told himself.

It was after sundown by the time he drew close enough to see his spread, in the darkness only a pair of lighted windows off in the distance. Molly would be worried, and he jiggled the reins, letting the horses know they could run a little if they still wanted to, and they did.

He covered the last mile and a half at near breakneck speed, slowing only when he knew the gate was near. He turned into the long lane leading to the ranch house, with the wheels sliding sideways on the sandy ground and the packages in the back of the wagon falling over on their sides. He heard something rolling, probably a tin, and glanced back to see if he was right, but it was too dark to be sure.

Molly heard the creak of the wagon and came out onto the porch as he pulled into the front yard. She was wringing her hands in her apron in that way she did when she was nervous. As he set the brake and looped the reins over the handle, she stepped off the porch.

"What happened? You're so late."

Dan didn't answer right away. He climbed down from the seat and walked to the rear of the wagon.

"I got your cloth," he said, leaning over the tailgate and grabbing the paper package.

She came close, then stood there, her hands hidden by the apron. "Is everything all right, Dan?"

He nodded. "Yeah. Everything's all right, Moll. There was a little trouble in town, but nothing to worry about."

"What kind of trouble?"

"Wes Fraser got himself shot."

"Shot? How horrible . . . is he all right?"

"I don't know. Doc Mitchell seemed to think maybe he'd pull through."

"Maybe? That's all, just maybe?"

"Yeah. That's all. Just maybe."

He handed her the package, and she looked at it without quite realizing what it was. Then she reached out, took hold, and wrapped her arms around it, clutching it to her chest. "Thanks. I almost forgot about it. I was so worried."

"Nothing to worry about. The children sleeping?"

"Yes. They wanted to wait up for you, but it was getting late, and I thought . . ."

She stopped, and Dan knew what it was she thought. She had a head full of fears, most of them outlandish, some of them downright laughable, and he had long since learned that when he couldn't tease her out of them, it was best to ignore them altogether. Molly was still not at home in the West. She was a farm girl through and through. And that was one of the things that preyed on his mind whenever the harsh realities of frontier living intruded on them. He couldn't build walls against those realities, but he didn't have to let them shape his life, either. But teaching Molly to look at things the same way was more than he had been able to accomplish.

"You go ahead on in," Brady said. "I'll bring the stuff in and put up the horses."

"Your supper's ready. Has been long since . . ."

"I'll be along directly, Moll."

He watched her turn and climb the steps to the porch, each foot seeming to hang an uncertain moment before it found the wooden stair she didn't quite seem to believe was right there waiting for it. When she was on the porch, she turned and stood there as he reached into the wagon for the groceries. He'd leave the nails in the wagon and drive over to the barn before unloading them.

He knew she was watching him, but he didn't want to say anything for fear of frightening her. There were a hundred questions swirling in the air all around her, questions she wanted to ask, questions for which she did not really want to know the answers, but which he would have to give her, whether she was ready or not.

He hoisted a sack of flour onto his shoulder and

walked toward the steps, taking them two at a time. She jerked open the screen door, almost as an afterthought, and he had to stop until it cleared him before moving into the house. Molly followed him in, and he dropped the flour sack in the pantry, waving away the small cloud of white dust it disgorged on impact.

He started back to the wagon, but Molly stood there, not quite in the way, but making her presence felt enough that he knew he was going to have to talk to her before he could finish with the wagon.

"I was there," he said. "I didn't see it, but I saw the men who probably did it."

"I see."

"The sheriff arrested one of them."

"How many were there?"

"Three. But I don't know what happened. I was outside. There was some sort of an argument, and it got out of hand, I guess. I heard the gunshot and went for the sheriff. When we got back, Mr. Fraser was on the floor, and so was one of the men. They were both unconscious."

"Who was he?"

"I don't know, some cowboy. Cody Fallon, his name is. Works for Clayton Riddle. All three of them do."

"Why did they do it? Why did they shoot Mr. Fraser?"

"I don't know, Molly. Like I said, there was an

argument." He shrugged his shoulders, an expression of his helplessness, both to explain the shooting and to protect her from knowing about it.

"We should have stayed in Ohio, Dan."

"Too late for that now, Moll. Way too late."

He finished his chores, put up the horses, and came back to the house. She had heated his food and was sitting across the table from his place. He sat down, rolling his cuffs down after having washed up at the well.

He ate quickly, not wanting to talk about the shooting, and not wanting, either, to sit there and have her eyes boring into him like a pair of augers. He tried once or twice to smile, thinking maybe he could ease her out of her mood, but it was useless. She'd have to sleep on it, get used to the idea. It would be all right in the morning, he thought.

They spent the rest of the meal in silence, Molly paying more attention to her fingers than anything else, brushing away crumbs that weren't there on her side of the table, cocking her ear toward the window for the most ordinary sound, as if it represented a threat she had never considered. But there was nothing Dan could do to ease her mind. Time was his only ally. And he couldn't help but wonder whether there was enough.

6

BRADY COULDN'T SLEEP. Instead, he sat on the porch, rolled a cigarette, and watched the sky. The bulky shadow of the half-finished barn looked like a slab of dark stone. When the moon peeked over the horizon, the raw timbers turned gray, somewhere between pewter and lead. All but the very brightest stars disappeared. He could see far beyond the barn, past the fence, and across the valley, where everything slowly dissolved. It was cool, and there was a bit of a wind, but he ignored the chill. Sucking the smoke into his lungs, he found himself thinking about a past he thought he had left behind. And it now seemed like a curse that he had managed so well.

He'd worked hard for what he had, and though it wasn't much, he knew that it could be, if only . . . what? The question echoed in his mind several times before he knew it was there, and when it finally insisted that he answer it, he voiced it aloud. And he had to admit that he didn't know the answer. There was no reason that things should change just because he happened to be outside Wes Fraser's store that afternoon, none that made any sense. But he couldn't shake the feeling that something, maybe even everything, had.

He got to his feet, holding the creaky rocking chair with one hand to keep it from making too much noise or banging against the wall behind him as he stood up. Stepping off the porch, he walked toward the barn, got halfway, then turned to look at the house. Everything that mattered to him was inside. Molly, her face probably softer than it had been when she'd gone to bed, the questions rattling around in her skull momentarily stilled, would be sleeping, or so he hoped.

The children, unaware that anything had happened, would be dreaming of castles and wild Indians, mixing them together in that bubbling cauldron where hopes and fears disguised themselves as one another. Brian who just that morning had said he wanted to be a soldier when he grew up, was probably holding off a horde of Apaches singlehandedly, a mound of spent cartridges beside him, the bright copper glittering like gold in the sunlight.

Kathleen was probably playing the piano in

her dreams. She'd been smitten by her first
glimpse of one at Ray Berry's, and had hung like
an appendage from Rachel Berry's apron strings
as she played everything from Beethoven to
Stephen Foster, translating the tiny black balls on
her sheet music into sounds Kathleen had never
heard before. It was a kind of magic for his
daughter, who had stabbed one tiny pink finger
at a note and asked what it sounded like, then
another and another, interrupting, to Rachel's
amusement, a rendering of Beethoven's 14th
Piano Sonata.

That such disparate things could coexist was
perhaps less amazing than it seemed at first glance.
Brady had seen starker contradictions in one man,
and, truth to tell, suspected they lay in every man,
not least himself. Now, the house bathed in the
light of a partial moon, everything looked picture
perfect. The curtains in the front window were
whiter, the walls of the house needed no paint, and
the wilted flowers that Molly tended with more
fervor than success seemed almost to thrive against
the raw timbers of the porch.

This was his life, he thought, a life that was not
as good as he had hoped for, but better, he suspected, than he deserved. Taking one final drag on
the cigarette, he tossed it to the ground, crushed it
under the toe of a boot, and walked past the barn,
tracking the fence with one hand, ignoring the stab

of splinters and the gluey sap beginning to coat his
fingers, making them stick together.

On the hillside, already fenced in, two dozen
horses bobbed their heads, tugging at the grass,
switched their tails and nickered nervously as they
sensed him approaching. At the fence, he stopped,
braced his elbows on the top rail, and watched
them, aware only of the grass all around them and
the threatening shadow now stopped nearby.
Under the moon, their coats glistened, and the
huge eyes of one stallion glowed like coals with the
reflected light.

Brady smiled to himself, patted the fence, and
turned his back to the animals to look at the house,
a quarter-mile away. It looked now like he had
hoped it would, neat, clean, pretty as a picture. He
felt the tug at the corners of his mouth, knowing
that the moonlight was better than a lie to hide the
truth, but knowing, too, that it didn't matter.
Nothing was perfect, not in his life, not in that of
anyone he knew.

Even Ray Berry, who, next to Clay Riddle, had
the largest spread in the valley, had complaints. It
seemed the natural order of things, somehow, and
it was pride of sinful proportions to believe you
were different, somehow better, that you deserved
more than others had. And Brady was not a pride-
ful man. He worked for what he had, and, since he
didn't believe in a God to thank, thanked instead

his lucky stars, and accepted the bad with the good. He wanted more, wanted perfection, wanted Molly to be happy, the children to be strong and healthy, but he knew his limits, knew there was just so much he could do. The rest, they would have to find somewhere inside themselves. If he kept them safe, it would be a small triumph. And, triumph or no, it would have to be enough.

Brady knew that he would have to testify against Fallon and the others. And he knew that if Wes Fraser didn't pull through, it would be his word against that of three men, men who would at the very least have no reason to tell the truth, men who would have every reason to want to see him dead to protect their own skins. So he had ample reason to want to see Fraser survive. It seemed a little selfish to him, caring more about his own troubles than those of the storekeeper, but that's the way it was. You came first, you and yours, then friends, then acquaintances, then strangers. It was like the rings on a target, and the points were awarded the same way—the closer to the center, the better the score, the more important it was. Wes Fraser was not on the bullseye. He wasn't a close friend, but more than an acquaintance. How did you quantify such things? How can you award points like that? he wondered.

He looked up at the moon, pale, staring back at him like a half-closed eye, as if waiting to see what he would do. And he didn't know. The uncertainty bothered him, but all he could do was wait, see what happened to Fraser and, when the time came, he would decide.

For a moment, he thought about rolling another cigarette, but didn't really want one, didn't know, really, what he wanted. He turned once more to look at the horses, then started back to the house, really feeling the chill now. On the grass under his feet, dew sparkled dully, like cloudy diamonds, and he bent to run his fingers through the blades, moistening his fingertips and rubbing them together, trying to harden the gummy sap from the fence rails, and rub it away on his jeans.

By the time he reached the house, he realized how tired he was, felt the weight of the day on his shoulders, and a tightness across his back and chest. He felt like the coiled spring in an over-wound clock. Stretching as he climbed up the steps, he shook his cuffs free of the dew and went inside without looking back.

In the bedroom, he sat on a chair to take off his boots, then tugged off his jeans. He walked to the bed then and stood looking down at Molly for a long moment, her face bathed in the moonlight. Even in sleep, he could see the tightness in her jaw. She was the same woman he'd married, had the same quiet beauty, but she was different somehow, too. Her face was still soft, but there was a hard-

ness beneath it, harder even than bone, as if the
beauty were a mask, one she wore to please him.
Maybe, he thought, we can sell the place and go
back East. They could talk about it in the morning.

He lowered himself to the bed as carefully as he
could, trying not to wake her, then lay back with
his arms folded behind his head, staring at the ceiling. Tired as he was, he knew sleep would be difficult. He turned on one hip to look at Molly,
reached out with one tentative hand to pull aside a
few strands of her dark hair that straggled across
her cheek. She moved, as if aware of him, but did
not open her eyes. For a moment, he wanted to kiss
her, but knew it would wake her and knew that she
would probably misunderstand his purpose.

He lay back then, closed his eyes, and tried to
sleep. Eventually, he knew, sleep would come. He
drifted off, felt himself floating, or falling, he
wasn't sure which, knew only that he was in mid-
air, nothing beneath him but blackness and uncertainty.

He heard the thump and sat up, not sure what it
was he'd heard. He glanced at the window. The
moon was gone now, and the sky was pale gray. It
was near sunrise.

Brady got to his feet and walked toward the
front of the house. Another thump, something
heavy and soft slamming into the porch, stopped
him in his tracks. He went to the window and

peered out without pulling aside the curtains. In the front yard, two men sat on horseback, dark gray against the lighter gray of the sky. It was too dark to see their faces clearly, but he didn't really have to see—he knew who they were.

Taking his Winchester from its rack over the fireplace, he walked to the door, opened it, and peered out through the screen. For one giddy moment, he thought about opening fire, killing the men and his problem in the same explosive burst, but the temptation passed, and he pushed open the screen and stepped out, pulling the inner door closed behind him.

He was barefoot, and the porch timbers were cold. Keeping his eyes fixed on the two riders, he stepped forward, bringing the rifle to bear. He felt something cold and wet squish between his toes, slipped, and fell heavily on the porch.

The two men laughed as a familiar smell swirled around him. He rolled over, felt something sop through the top of his long johns, and nearly gagged. He got up, instinctively brushing the horseshit from his underwear, and cursed under his breath.

"You got a big mouth, Brady," one of them, it sounded like Don Gallup, said.

"Get off my land!"

Gallup ignored him. "Cody Fallon's in jail, and that ain't right. You put him there."

"I told you to get off my land, dammit." Brady levered a round into the Winchester's chamber and moved to the edge of the porch. "Now get out, before I lose my temper."

"You ain't gonna shoot, Brady. Got no cause. You don't want to end up in a cell next to Cody, do you?"

"He's right where he belongs. You ought to be there with him."

"That right? What makes you say so?"

"What happened to Wes Fraser, that's what makes me say so."

"Don't know nothing about that."

"You were there. You were arguing with him. You know what happened as well as I do. Better than I do, in fact."

"Oh, and just what might it be that we know, Brady?"

"I won't dignify that with an answer. Now, you get on away from here and leave me be. I'm going to count to ten, and if you aren't moving, I'll move you myself."

"Look kinda comical, horseshit all over your drawers and all. Seems like maybe you ain't the man to move nobody, least of all me."

"You think so, you just sit right there. One . . . two . . ."

"You best think about what you seen and what you didn't see, Brady. You don't want to be mixin' in where you got no business mixin'. You got a nice little place here . . . nice family . . . pretty wife, too."

"Three . . ."

"Pity if you was to lose all that."

"You threatening me?"

"Seems like you stopped counting."

"Four . . ."

Gallup laughed, slid from the saddle, and walked toward the porch. "You listen to me, Brady, and you hear what I say. You keep your goddamned mouth shut. Ain't nobody but you says Cody had anything to do with what happened to Fraser. You didn't see nothing, so you'd be better off keeping your mouth shut nice and tight."

"Five . . ."

Gallup was standing right below him now, his nose more or less level with the muzzle of the Winchester. "You think you got the sand to pull the trigger, you go right on ahead. But I don't think you do."

"Six . . . seven . . . eight . . ."

Gallup turned to his partner then. "What do you think, Jimmy? You think he's got the balls to pull that trigger?"

"Nine . . ."

"Naw, I don't think so. He don't want no trouble."

"Ten!"

Gallup leaned forward, reached up for the barrel

of the carbine, and tugged it toward his chest. "There," he said. "Nice and close. You can't miss from that range. Go ahead, pull the trigger, Brady."

Brady heard something behind him then. "Molly?" he called, without taking his eyes off Gallup. "Molly, you stay inside."

"What's wrong, Dan? What's happening?" She pushed open the door, and he knew he wasn't going to shoot, not now, not with her standing there in the open doorway. Deep in his gut, he knew he wouldn't have pulled the trigger anyway, even if she hadn't come out.

"Nothing's wrong. Go on back inside."

Gallup took off his hat. "Morning, Missus Brady," he said.

"Dan, who are these men?"

"You think about what I said, Brady," Gallup said then clapped his hat back on and turned his back. Anderson sat on his horse, chuckling while Gallup walked slowly back to his mount, swung up into the saddle, and jerked the reins.

They were gone a moment later when Molly stepped out onto the porch. "Who was that, Dan? What's that smell?"

"Horseshit," he said. "That answers both of your questions."

7

THE BRADYS ATE BREAKFAST in silence. Molly
had said nothing about the early morning visitors,
but Dan knew they were on her mind. Every time
she looked at him, he could see the questions in her
eyes: Why did they come? What did they want?
And he knew that she knew the answer as well as
he did. The more important question was what to
do about it.

To avoid frightening the children, Dan resolved
to keep silent, not even to tell Molly what he
planned to do. The less they knew, the better.
Brian, at six, would get excited, have his head
swell with exalted scenarios about bad men and
heroes. His imagination was full enough as it was
of such notions, and Dan, who never spoke about
his time in uniform, had done nothing to disabuse
the boy, as much because it was too painful to re-

member as because he knew it would do no good.
Brian was a six-year-old boy, and there was no
talking to a youngster that age about death and violence. It was all just pictures in a book, and the
smell of gunpowder never came off the printed
page, and blood was black, not red, and didn't
steam in the cold air.

As for Kathleen, Brady would give his life to
keep her from harm. He wanted her to flit through
her days like a butterfly, dancing from flower to
flower in a world full of sunlight and sweet fragrance. He did not want to be the one to fill her
sleep with monsters on horseback. All of that was
unspoken, but not unacknowledged in the glances
that passed between Dan and Molly as they ate
their morning meal.

But Dan knew that the best way to keep control
of the situation was to make the first move. His
only problem was deciding what that move ought
to be. Not that he had so many options. When the
dishes were cleared away from the table, he sent
the children outside to play and waited for Molly
to voice the questions he knew were the only
things on her mind.

After puttering with the dishes, washing them in
the wooden tub, and wiping them dry, she sat
down at the table, a cup of coffee in front of her.
Her hands sat on either side of the cup like al-
abaster bookends. The long fingers, piano fingers

he called them, seemed restless, but the hands never moved. She looked at him directly for the first time since sunup. "What are you going to do?" she asked.

There it was. And he had to tell her the truth. He'd never once lied to her, not since the first time he'd laid eyes on her, and he wasn't about to start now. "I don't know."

"If Wes Fraser dies, you'll be the only witness," she said. "Won't you?"

Brady shrugged. "Not much of a witness, really. I mean I didn't see the shooting. I don't think it will make much difference in court."

"Those men think so, though."

"Yes, they do."

"Did they threaten you?"

He shook his head, then looked out the window. He could see Brian and Kathleen walking along the fence, and when they reached the unfinished end, Brian stuck out a hand and let it rest on the final post, a miniature man surveying his day's work. Kathleen seemed less concerned about the fence, if she thought about it at all, and moved into the grass, bent over, and plucked a buttercup and held it under her chin. She must have said something to Brian, because the boy turned, gave her a funny look, then leaned forward to look at Kathleen's neck where, Brady knew, the yellow reflection of the flower would have given her skin a jaundiced look.

Brian held out his hand, took the flower, and held it up to his own chin, jutting his jaw forward to give maximum exposure to the flower.

But the question was still there in the air, hanging like smoke, motionless, waiting. Brady took a deep breath. "No, they didn't threaten me. They didn't have to, really. They knew I would know why they were here. That was the point of their visit, after all, to make the possibility of violence real, in case it hadn't occurred to me."

"You'll have to testify against that man Fallon, won't you?"

"I suppose so. I guess it depends on what the circuit judge does when he gets here. But if they call me, I'll have to tell them what I saw, precious little though it was."

"And will you?"

"Will I what?"

"Testify?"

"How can I not? I was there. I got the sheriff. I saw what I saw and heard what I heard. How would it look if I were to walk away from that? I mean, Wes Fraser is lying there in Doc Mitchell's infirmary fighting for his life. I can't just pretend that didn't happen."

"Of course not." She got up then, and Brady could tell by the set of her shoulders that she wasn't happy but was not prepared to discuss either the breadth or the depth of that unhappiness, at least not for the moment. He didn't blame her. He understood her desire to be left alone, to live as if they were the only people on earth. That was, after all, part of the reason they had come West, because it was his desire as much as, maybe even more than, hers. But it wasn't that simple. Not now.

Brady walked over to Molly, where she stood looking out the window at the children. He put his arm around her, felt the stiffness of her back, and ignored it long enough to squeeze. "It'll be all right, Moll. You'll see."

He didn't expect her to answer, and he wasn't surprised. He went outside then, walking toward the barn with the gait of a man who isn't sure where he's going, or if he wants to go at all. Inside the barn, he gathered his tools together, laid them in a pile beside the new keg of nails, then knelt down. He pried open the keg, put on his dirty canvas apron, and stuffed the pockets of the apron with nails.

Picking up the tools, he went outside and walked along the fence. Brian heard him coming and raced toward him. "Can I help today, Dad?" he called.

Brady knelt as his son approached. "Not today, son. I think maybe you ought to spend the day with your sister. Besides, it won't be long before the day comes when you start working for real, and that'll be it for the rest of your life. Might as well enjoy your freedom while you have it."

Brian didn't look as if he had been convinced, but when Brady straightened up, he didn't argue, skipped toward the house, and called to Kathleen to follow him. Brady watched them go, then walked the rest of the way along the fence. He took off his apron, dropped it on the ground, and grabbed a fence post. The fence line was marked by a series of cones of earth, dried now and pale beige under the morning sun.

He dropped the post into the hole, walked back to the pile, and hoisted another. After an hour, he had twenty in place. But he still had to fill in the earth around them, pack it tight, then put the rails in and nail them securely. He knew that most ranchers didn't bother with the nails, but it seemed to him that letting the rails sit loose, even though the overlapping tongues acted as shims to hold each other in place, was too temporary, as if the fence were no more permanent than a tipi frame, something you picked up and carried away at a moment's notice. And he wanted something that would last.

Sometimes, the sweat dripping down his back, running into his eyes from drenched hair, the salt stinging his eyes and blurring his vision, he wondered whether he was afraid of his own impermanence. Maybe, he would think, there is something in me that doesn't know how to stay put. Maybe I'm afraid that I'll pack up and move on, miss my main chance because I'm too damned afraid to stay where I am and see what happens. He'd dismiss the suspicion, waving it away angrily, like a man chasing a bee, but it came too often and stayed too long for him to ignore it.

Back at the barn, he grabbed his shovel. Stopping at the well for a dipper of water, he removed his hat and raised the dipper, pouring half of it over his head and letting it run down inside his shirt to cool him off a bit. He toed the small muddy craters the dripping water made in the dust, clapped his hat back on, and strode with more energy than purpose back to the fence.

Leaning the shovel against his hip, he positioned the first post in the center of its hole, eyeballing it for vertical alignment, and used his feet to fill the hole with enough loose dirt to hold the post in place. He packed the dirt evenly with the shovel and then used his weight to compact it even more tightly. He worked his way along the line until he'd finished with all of the posts he had dropped in place. Then he squatted behind the last and sighted along the row of poles to see how close he'd come to perfect alignment. One or two were slightly off kilter, but they were none of them bad enough to require redoing, and he took a deep breath, like a man narrowly avoiding a bullet.

It was nearly time for lunch, and he looked at the house, squinting in the sunlight, wondering what kind of mood Molly would be in. He hated having to wonder, hated, too, that he could make a reasonable guess, hated himself for knowing and for putting her in the position she was in. But the truth was, he didn't know what else to do.

As he started toward the porch, beyond the house, he saw the road stretching away toward town, and on the crest of a hill, a lone rider heading toward him. For a moment, he stood still, squinting against the glare, trying to recognize the solitary figure, but with the harsh light and the sweat in his eyes, it was impossible.

Galvanized by recollection of the early morning visit, he broke into a run, tossing the shovel aside and wiping his eyes with his sleeve. The heat hammered down on him, and he was soaked to the skin from his morning's labor. Dust swirled in the air and clung to the glaze of perspiration on his skin. He reached the front yard and pounded up the steps and into the house.

Molly was just putting a plate of potatoes on the table, and stared at him, the plate hovering inches above the table top.

"What's wrong?"

"Nothing, I hope. Somebody's coming."

"Oh, Dan!"

"Don't worry about it. Just stay inside. Keep Brian and Kathleen inside, too."

He grabbed his Winchester from the rack and bounded around the table and back onto the porch. Stepping down into the yard, he saw the rider, much closer now, but no more recognizable. He started down the lane toward the road, hoping to meet whoever it was as far away from the house as possible.

The rider saw him and waved one hand over his head. It was a disarming gesture, and Brady relaxed a bit, but still kept on sprinting. He reached the road while the rider was still three hundred yards away. Instinctively, he looked back at the house. Molly was at the window, the curtain bunched in one hand, her eyes shielded against the sun by the other.

Blinking once more, Brady saw the features of the unknown visitor gradually resolve into those of Matt Lowry.

The sheriff pulled up fifty yards away, walked his horse the last bit, and slid from the saddle.

"Dan," he said. "Bad news."

"What is it? What's happened? Wes . . . ?"

Lowry nodded. "Died early this morning, just past sunup. Doc done everything he could, but Wes had just lost too much blood."

"Jesus Christ!"

Lowry rubbed his lips with the back of his hand, then licked them with a dry tongue. "Never did regain consciousness," he said. "Not one blamed word."

Brady expelled his breath in a rush, only then realizing that he'd been holding it in. "Damn, I'm sorry, Matt. How's Sarah taking it?"

"About like you'd expect. I got to tell you, I'm a little worried about you, Dan."

"Why me?"

"Because you're the only witness, Dan, the only one who has a chance of puttin' the blame on the right shoulders. I don't know if your testimony'll be good enough, but one thing's sure, and that's that we don't have a chance in hell without it of seeing to it that those murdering bastards pay for what they done."

Brady pushed his hat back, rubbed a fingertip in the pasty film on his forehead, then wiped the fingertip on his jeans. "Maybe there's no point in even trying, Matt. Maybe you ought to just cut Fallon loose and . . ."

"Christ, man, you can't mean that!"

"You said it yourself, Matt, my testimony is pretty feeble."

"All the same, Dan, I . . ."

"I had a couple of visitors this morning."

Lowry furrowed his brow. "What are you talking about?"

"Gallup and Anderson. They threw some horse apples on my front porch, and when I came out to see what the rumpus was, they as much as told me to forget about testifying."

"And you intend to do what they told you, is that it?"

"I don't know. Maybe it'd be best."

Lowry spat off to the side, licked his lips again, and looked Brady square in the eye. "Wes Fraser was a good man, Dan. You know that. He don't deserve what happened to him. He was a friend to a lot of folks in these parts. And it don't seem right nobody wants to be a friend to him now, when it don't do him no good."

"I have a family to worry about, Sheriff."

"You let Gallup and Fallon and them get away with this, you might as well pack up your family and move on. There won't be no place for children in this valley, nor women neither. Not if cold-blooded murder don't mean nothing."

"I'll have to think about it, Sheriff. When do you expect the judge?"

"Two, three days. No more'n that."

"I'll let you know."

He turned then and started back toward the house. He could feel the twin gimlets of Lowry's gaze boring into his back with every step. He wanted to turn, to tell the sheriff that of course he would testify. But he didn't know whether he would have meant it or not. He needed time, time to sort things out, time to decide. A little time, that's all.

8

BRADY FELT LIKE he'd let Lowry down. More than that, he felt as if he'd let himself down, in some way that he could not identify. Looking into his own heart, he saw nothing, as if he were an empty well, hollow, full only of echoes and dead air.

He watched the sheriff ride back the way he'd come, never once looking back, never slowing, until horse and rider both vanished over the same ridge where Brady had first seen them. Only when the sheriff was out of sight did Brady loosen his grip on the Winchester, let it slide butt first along his leg and thump against the ground.

Without looking at the house, he knew Molly was watching him, and he found it hard to turn. Knowing that he would have to tell her sooner or later, he heaved a sigh, shaking his head as if in re-

sponse to a question in the air, and walked down
the lane, thumping the carbine against his leg with
every step. Harder and harder, he cracked the
heavy stock into his calf until it made him wince,
then he looked down at the gun as if surprised it
was there at all.

He looked at the house then, saw Molly in the
doorway, and hefted the gun to hang from a
crooked elbow. When he reached the yard, she
came out onto the porch, her lips pursed sourly
around the question that echoed in her dark eyes.
"That was Matt Lowry, wasn't it?"

"Yes."

"What did he want?"

Brady wrestled with the knowledge, tried to
shape it into something soft, palatable, but the
hard truth was not malleable, and finally, he let it
out plain and unvarnished. "Wes Fraser's dead,"
he told her. "He died early this morning."

"I see," she said, bobbing her head like an irate
schoolmarm. "Those men this morning, they knew
that, didn't they?"

Brady shook his head. "I don't think so. Lowry
said Fraser passed around sunup. They were already here by then."

"But they knew, all the same. They knew he was
going to die."

"I suppose."

"What did the sheriff want you to do?"

"What do you think he wanted, Moll? He wanted me to know, because he knew it would have some influence on what I tell the judge . . ."

"What's the point in telling the judge anything, now? That man Fallon will get off. You know that. All you can do is bring trouble. What's the point of testifying? Those men threatened you. They threatened us. Did you tell him that?"

"I told him."

"And what did he say?"

"Not much." Brady hesitated for a moment, then decided to confide his own reluctance. "I also told him I didn't know whether there was any point in testifying. I told him I didn't see enough to convict Fallon or the others."

"He tried to talk you into it, did he?"

"That's his job, Moll."

"No, his job is to protect innocent people from the likes of those riffraff. And he's not doing much of a job of it, either, is he?"

"It's not his fault."

"Well, it's not our fault, either." She turned, made as if to go back inside, then stopped. With her back to him, she leaned against the doorframe. In a voice that was barely audible, she said, "I'm frightened, Dan. I don't know what . . . I don't mean to sound like I don't care about Mr. Fraser. I do. I feel awful. Poor Sarah. What will she do?"

Brady climbed the steps and leaned the Winchester against the wall. He circled his arms around Molly's waist, leaned his head on her shoulder, wallowing in the luxuriant wash of her hair. "It'll be all right, honey. Try not to worry."

She nodded her head uncertainly, but said nothing. She extricated herself from his grasp and went inside. Brady followed her, licking his lips and looking for some additional words to stiffen her, to help her find the confidence they would both need in the next few days. But the words weren't there.

He watched her go inside, not knowing whether he wanted to follow her. He sat on the steps then, his back curved as if under a great weight, staring at the toes of his boots. He knew that Molly was right to be frightened, but he had to find some way not to let her fear become his. Terror was like a communicable disease, and if he caught it, then they would have no chance at all to live a normal life in Nogales. They would spend the rest of their lives in secret shame, knowing that they should have done something and, in choosing not to, had given a nod of silent approval to the killing of Wes Fraser.

Dan Brady was not a coward, but now he was not so sure that made a difference. He also understood that he couldn't do something rash just to prove to himself that his courage had not deserted him. There was Molly to think about, and the children. If he did something foolish, got himself killed, they would suffer.

He kept thinking back to the moment of the shooting, wondering if there was something he could have done. But every time he sifted through those last few moments before he heard the gunshot, he came to the same conclusion—there was nothing he could have done, nothing that wouldn't have given events a push and sent them sliding downhill even faster than they finally had.

He went in to get something to eat, not really hungry, not really wanting to sit across the table from Molly because he knew the question would still be there in her eyes—a question he had no answer for, none that convinced him. And if he didn't believe his own answer, then it was certain that Molly wouldn't believe it either.

But he couldn't hide from the question, so he got slowly to his feet, stretched, tried to compose his features in some semblance of serenity, and walked inside. Molly was waiting for him, as he knew she would be. The children had already eaten, and Molly sent them outside with a list of chores guaranteed to keep them out of harm's way for at least an hour.

They ate in silence. It was like that deep quiet that usually followed an argument, but even more profound, when every movement filled the room with the whisper of cloth on cloth, every twisting joint snapped like a log on a fire. He wanted to break it, but had nothing to say, and he knew she knew it. Words would have seemed artificial, not quite lies, but not quite genuine, either. It was better to listen to the sounds of their own bodies trying to be still, trying to eat without making rude noises, their eyes darting this way and that, never quite making contact with each other's.

An idea began to take shape in his mind as he ate. It was crazy, maybe, but it seemed like the only chance he had to avoid letting events take charge of him. If he didn't do something, he would find himself as helpless as a leaf on a flood, buffeted by whatever came along, unable to control where he went or what happened to him when he got there. He let it simmer through the meal, and by the time he pushed his empty plate away, he still hadn't found an alternative that offered him any better chance of success.

Over coffee, he debated whether to tell Molly, knowing she would disapprove, but knowing that she would be angry if he did something without telling her first. So he told her, because he couldn't think of a way not to.

"I'm going to talk to Clay Riddle this afternoon, he said. He let the words hang there, simple, matter of fact. If she asked him why, he would tell her, but under the table he crossed his fingers, hoping she would just let it go.

She sipped her own coffee, pursing her lips against the hot liquid, sipping daintily. The tip of her tongue teased out between her lips for a moment, and he could see the small, even white teeth so perfect that she was the envy of every woman in Nogales, for that one thing alone. Finally, she nodded her head, a movement so slight it might have been imagined. Then came the question he was hoping she wouldn't ask. "Why?"

"He was there when Wes Fraser got shot. Cody Fallon works for him. So do the other two men."

"The men who were here?" And when he nodded his head yes, she added, "The same two men who were arguing with Mr. Fraser, the ones who were in the store?"

"Yes."

"And what do you expect Clay Riddle to do? What can he do? If Matt Lowry didn't see fit to arrest them, what do you think talking to Clay Riddle will accomplish?"

"I'll ask him to talk to Gallup and Anderson. Tell them to leave us be."

She laughed without amusement. "Dan, Riddle won't do anything. There's nothing he can do. Those men won't listen to him anyway. And if you . . ."

He slammed the table. "Dammit, Moll, I've got to do something!"

"Dan, we didn't ask for this trouble. But now it's come, and we just have to ride it out."

"I won't live like a goddamned mole. I won't

allow them to buffalo me. We live here, and we have a right to go where we choose, do what we want."

Molly got up, leaving her half-empty cup on the table, and walked to the window. She pushed aside the curtain and looked at the yard. She didn't say anything, but he knew what she was doing. She was checking on the children, not to see that they were busy at their assigned chores so much as to see that they were all right.

When she let the curtain drop, she didn't turn around. "Maybe it wouldn't hurt to talk to Mr. Riddle," she said. Her voice lacked conviction, and there was an undercurrent of desperation in the near whisper.

She turned to him, folded her arms across her waist, and leaned back against the window sill. "You be careful."

He got up then, moved out from behind the table, and walked toward her. "I'm sorry for all this," he said.

She gave him a half-hearted smile. "I know," she said. "I know that. And I don't blame you. It's not your fault. I'm just confused. I know you have to testify against Fallon. There's nothing else you can do. But I don't have to like it."

She gave him a long look, and he could sense the weight of things tugging at her face, making her cheeks sag just a little. He reached out and touched her cheek, letting his work-hardened palm rest against the cool, smooth skin. "Things'll work out," he said. "If I have anything to say about it."

She stiffened then, and he thought for a moment she was going to remind him just how little he actually had to say about it, but if the thought crossed her mind, she suppressed it. She nodded her head. "I know," she said.

"I guess I'll do a little more work on the barn before I go. I'm tired of fence work. It'll be a change." He smiled, and it felt genuine for the first time in two days. She smiled back, but he wasn't sure she meant it. She wanted things to be easy for him, easier than they were. As hard as it was on her living so far from what she knew, it was just as hard on him, and she knew it. But she didn't like to complain because she knew the work itself was burden enough for him.

He went outside, called to Brian, and watched his son scamper toward him, dust streaking his cheeks, his tiny legs pumping. The boy had his face and Molly's body. He would be short, most likely, like her father and her uncles, but well made, strong through the chest and shoulders.

Brian bounced up the steps with a stumble and landed on his knees. "Found a snake, Dad," he said. "A big one."

"Where? What kind?" Brady immediately envisioned a diamondback. "Where's your sister?"

"She's watching it. She has a stick and keeps poking it."

Brady started to run.

"It's not poison, Dad. It's not a rattler. Don't worry."

Brady, not sure Brian knew a rattler from a garter snake, didn't slow down. By the time he reached Kathleen, his breath was exploding from his lungs with every step. He found her with a long stick in hand, an angry snake at bay against a pile of fence posts. It was hissing in annoyance every time Kathleen made a feint with the stick.

"Kathy, stop that!" Brady snapped, his voice harder than he had meant.

"It's just a stupid old snake, Daddy," she said.

Brady looked closer and saw that it was, indeed, relatively harmless. Instead of the poisonous serpent he'd expected, Kathleen had cornered a good-sized kingsnake, a six-footer from the look of it, its brown bands so dark they were almost black as coal even in the bright sunlight.

"I don't think he cares to have you pokin' him like that," Brady said.

"Can I keep him?"

Brady took the stick from her hand. "No, honey. There's no place to keep him."

"But I like him, Daddy."

"Maybe we can find you another snake, Kath. A smaller one."

"Promise?" He could tell from her voice that she wasn't convinced she wanted any snake but this one, but he was firm.

"I promise."

"When?"

"Soon as we can find one."

"Today?"

Brady laughed. "Okay, we'll look later, all right? You go on back to the house while we let this fellow go on his way."

Kathleen walked halfway to the house backward, and only when Brady backed away and the kingsnake slithered along the bottom of the lumber pile and turned the corner did she turn around.

Brady watched it go, chewing on his lower lip. He was thinking of another snake, and hoping this one didn't bring as much trouble. He already had more than he wanted.

9

AT FOUR O'CLOCK, Brady put down his hammer and stood back to look at the barn. One wall to go, he thought. And with any luck, he'd have it done in a couple of days. He took off his tool apron and walked toward the door, ducked inside, and tossed the apron without looking. It thumped against a nail keg, and the hollow sound bounced off the roof high overhead. And it reminded him of Wes Fraser. If only he had listened to Wes in the first place, he'd have bought more nails the first time and wouldn't have been within five miles of the store when Fraser had been shot.

The thought made him feel a little selfish. But that was spilled milk. Or spilled blood, he thought. He walked to the corral and saddled his horse, then went inside to tell Molly he was leaving. He took the Winchester from its place over the mantel, and she scowled at him, but said nothing. "Be back in a couple of hours," he said.

She followed him to the door, and when he climbed into the saddle, she was still there, one hand on the doorframe, the other curled over her chin as if she was trying to remember something. She waved, and he waved back. Then he wheeled the big chestnut stallion around and clucked. "Come on, Chester." He flapped his knees against the stallion's sides. The name embarrassed him, but he was stuck with it. He had asked Brian to name the horse, never expecting the boy would come up with something so inappropriate, but a deal was a deal.

When he reached the end of the lane, he glanced back over his shoulder, half expecting to see Molly still in the doorway, like some statue, but she had gone back inside. He was glad, thinking that maybe she had gotten over her nervousness, at least a little.

It was a good three-quarters of an hour to Clay Riddle's spread, and he wanted to be there with plenty of sun, because he had no idea how his visit, and the request that prompted it, would be received by the rancher. As he rode, he tried to frame a way to ask Riddle for help that wouldn't seem like an admission of either weakness or cowardice, but the truth was, he felt weak and cowardly, and no matter what he said, that was going to gnaw at him. Still, it seemed the only way open to him.

Riddle was a decent man and, in all likelihood, would be called to testify at the hearing because he had been there when Fraser and Fallon were found. He was also there when Fallon was arrested and, although he had offered to be responsible for the young hand, hadn't pressed it when Matt Lowry said no. They were in the same boat, really, and Riddle would do the honorable thing.

But Riddle hadn't been there when the shots were fired. He hadn't seen the argument, and he hadn't heard the breaking glass, which, in retrospect, suggested, but didn't prove, that Gallup and Anderson escaped through the back door of Fraser's store. Brady knew that without him and his testimony, Riddle's story wouldn't be anywhere near enough to warrant holding Fallon for trial.

It was a beautiful late afternoon. The sun was still high in the sky, and masses of cumulus drifted across the brilliant blue like huge ships, flat-keeled and top-heavy. Watching them as he rode, Brady half expected them to topple over, their sails left to dangle like curtains nailed to a ceiling. There would be a great sunset later. The clouds guaranteed that, and he looked forward to seeing it on the ride home.

The Rolling R was a sprawling ranch, and Brady slowed at the sign marking the property line when he still had fifteen or twenty minutes to ride. Clay Riddle hadn't fenced his spread the way some of the ranchers had, and Brady wondered how many miles of barbed wire it would take to enclose so vast an expanse. Rails would have been far too expensive, but Riddle, like many of the larger ranchers, didn't really believe in fences anyway. He preferred his stock, horses and cattle alike, to range freely.

There was no one in sight, and he wondered whether Gallup and Anderson were out on the range or at the ranch house. Brady was nervous. He leaned forward to pat the stock of his Winchester, and found himself wondering whether he would have to start carrying a sidearm. He had a Colt .44 tucked away in a trunk, but the thought of strapping it on was not attractive.

He was moving uphill now, and knew that when he reached the top of the rise, the Riddle spread would fill the next valley. He slowed as he neared the crest of the hill, castigated himself for the delay, but still didn't nudge the horse to go faster. He wondered whether he was trying to postpone the inevitable, or if he was just plain scared. Either answer came down to the same thing.

At the top of the hill, he reined in, let his hands rest on the pommel of his saddle, the reins gripped loosely, and pushed his hat back. He was sweating. As he wiped his brow with a floppy kerchief tucked in his back pocket, he could see several horses in the corral alongside a barn that was three times the size of his own. The long, low bunkhouse, sparkling with whitewash, sported a chimney at either end, and one of them spouted a thin column of smoke, probably a small fire for coffee for the hands who were already in from the range.

A broad creek meandered through the valley, zigzagging its lazy way to the southwest. Its waters were cool, even in summer, and Brady had more than once caught a trout or two on one of Clay Riddle's occasional fishing picnics. Riddle loved fishing even more than ranching, and was one of the few ranchers in the area who could afford the leisure of a trip to the Sangre de Cristo mountains to the north for the sole and express purpose of, as he put it, "settin' on my ass a few days with nothin' to do but wettin' a string." A wooden bridge crossed the creek almost dead center, to accommodate wagons and the more fastidious riders, mostly women, who preferred not to plunge into the creek and wade their mounts across.

The centerpiece of the Rolling R was the main house. Two stories with a dozen large windows on each level, kept open in summer to make maximum use of the breeze. White lace curtains fluttered like the wings of moths on the second floor. At the center of the house, a broad porch, its roof supported by four neoclassical columns, their capitals ornately carved. Mary Jane Riddle had told him what they were—Doric, Ionic, he didn't remember—but recalled how crisp and precise the carvings were.

The house sat on a hilltop, lower than the one from which Brady admired it, and a smooth green lawn swept up from the valley floor, studded with clumps of pin-oaks and ash trees. Some huge stones that had been uncovered during the laying of the foundation had been muscled into clusters, and Mary Jane had spent much of her free time since the construction puttering with her rock garden. Ivy draped the huge rocks, spilled like green water down onto the lawn, and crept up several of the nearer trees. A walkway of whitewashed flagstones curled up the hillside in threes and fours where the ground had been carved into a series of long broad steps. Box hedge lined either side and grew chest high. As Brady watched, one of the hands hacked at the hedge with a pair of long-handled pruning shears, cutting away the recent growth and rediscovering the perfect symmetry Mrs. Riddle demanded of her vegetation.

Roses were planted at either end of the porch, some of them climbers, and they all but obscured a pair of fan-shaped trellises. The tall cones of junipers separated pairs of windows on the ground floor, their green almost black in the bright sunlight.

It was picture perfect, Brady thought, and for a

moment, he felt a twinge of envy. Clay Riddle had everything, everything a man could want, and everything Dan Brady had hoped to have when he drove the first nail into the raw timbers that were to become his own house.

For a moment, the brilliant white of the house was muted as the shadow of a huge cloud swept up the hill, darkening a swath two acres wide as it scudded before the wind. Instinctively, Brady glanced up at the sky, identified the offending cloud, and waited until the sun reappeared before he looked back at the house.

Knowing there was nothing to be gained by sitting on the hill like a goddamned fool, his chin glistening with an envious drool, he clapped his knees against the chestnut's side and nudged the horse forward and down the gentle slope to the valley floor. Far to his left, at one end of the broad valley, he could see brown clumps, cattle standing under cottonwoods and oaks to keep out of the sun. The ribbon of creek glittered like polished silver here and there, light splattering on the ripples and glancing off in every direction.

Brady headed for the bridge, figuring he'd have to go inside the main house and not wanting to muddy Mary Jane's carpet with his boots. When he reached the bridge, he stopped once more, just for a moment, then urged the chestnut across, listening to the drumming of its hooves on the raw timber.

He debated whether to tie off at the foot of the hill and walk up the flagstone path or move on around to the back and hitch at the bunkhouse rail. Knowing it was likely that Gallup or Anderson would be at the bunkhouse, he decided to take the front walk. Dismounting, he looped the reins around the rail, slipped from the saddle, and let his hand rest on the stock of the Winchester for a long moment. He looked at it, started to pull it from the boot, then let it slide back, patted it almost fondly, and started up the walk.

The man with the hedge clippers looked familiar and seemed to recognize him. Brady figured he must have seen the man around Nogales and nodded. The man nodded back, then started clipping the hedge again as Brady moved past, grunting with every snap of the heavy blades. It seemed to Brady that there was just a touch more vehemence in the clipping, as if something had annoyed the ranch hand, maybe being seen doing such tame and citified work or maybe Brady himself.

When he reached the top of the walk, the scent of roses wafted around him on the stiff breeze, and as he climbed up the steps of the imposing porch, he saw movement beyond the tall glass panels framing the doorway.

A moment later, Mary Jane Riddle stepped onto the porch, a white dress billowing around her. She was a pleasant woman, but considered a little snooty by most of the townspeople, mostly because of her exquisite manners and her unabashed affection for cultural refinements. The Riddle place was, so far as Brady knew, the only one for fifty miles in any direction that could boast of a grand piano, which Mary Jane Riddle played with considerable accomplishment. It was a piano that put Rachel Perry's battered upright to shame.

She smiled broadly. "Why, Mr. Brady, what brings you all the way out here?" She was small, and her features were delicate as a China doll's. Her complexion was unnaturally dark against the white dress.

"Missus Riddle, afternoon. Sorry to bother you, but I'd like to speak to Clay a minute, if I might."

"Of course, come on in. Come on in." She fluttered her hands in the air as if not quite sure what to do with them, then gestured for him to precede her into the house. "Clay's in his study," she said, then in a voice that seemed too large for so tiny a woman, she hollered, "Clay? Company . . ."

She swept past him, her dress billowing around her, and made an abrupt turn to the left so smoothly that she seemed to float. Brady quickened his pace and made the same left turn, down a hallway, where the last white flags of Mary Jane Riddle's dress were just vanishing through a doorway.

Riddle stepped into the hall then, a cigar clamped in his blocky jaw. "Dan," he said, "what can I do for you?"

Before Brady could answer, Riddle turned and said, "I think this is man talk, Margie, leave us alone for a few minutes, would you?"

She smiled. "Coffee, Mr. Brady?"

"No, thank you, Missus Riddle."

"All right, then, I'll leave you two to your conspiracy." She walked out as gracefully as she'd entered, and Riddle closed the door before walking to a huge desk and sitting on one corner of the gleaming walnut.

"What's on your mind, Dan?" he asked, opening a cigar box and extending it toward his visitor.

Brady shook his head. "No, thanks. Don't smoke anything but cigarettes."

Riddle set the box down and folded his hands in his lap. He looked at Brady, waiting for his guest to divulge the purpose of his visit. Brady cleared his throat.

"Had a couple of visitors early this morning," he began. "Don Gallup and Jim Anderson."

Riddle knit his brows. "Visit, you say? What for? They were supposed to be working. What'd they want?"

"They wanted to tell me not to testify at the hearing, whenever the judge gets here."

"They did, did they? What'd you tell 'em?"

"Not much. But it frightened Molly, and I was pretty angry about it myself."

"They threaten you, did they?" He nodded as if to answer his own question. "Can't say as I like that. Between you and me, I don't think Cody Fallon ought to be in jail. I can't see Cody shootin' nobody. Gallup, maybe, especially with a belly full of whiskey. But something sure as hell happened, and since Wes Fraser's passed, I guess it's up to you and me and Al Fisher to help the judge figure out what it was."

"You're going to testify, then?"

"Hell, yes. I don't know if those boys done anything, but if you held a gun to my head and made me say what I think, I'd say I think they done it. Trouble is, I didn't see nothing, and neither did you. Fact is, you're the only one can put them in the store at all, which makes you a pretty important man, as far as they're concerned. But don't worry about it. I'll talk to 'em, tell 'em to leave you be. It ain't up to nobody but the judge to say what happens next."

"I'd appreciate it, Clay."

"Hell, it's only right. Course, I can't go convicting 'em before the judge has his say. That's the only reason I haven't cut them loose already. But I won't stand for them threatening a neighbor, no matter whether they done anything else or not. They bother you again, you let me know, but I don't think they will. I'll read 'em the riot act for sure. Let's you and me go over to the bunkhouse right now, and get this straightened out."

Brady wasn't sure it was a good idea, but he didn't want Riddle to think he was frightened of Gallup. He nodded. "All right. If you think it's a good idea."

Riddle laughed. He sensed Brady's uneasiness, and said, "Hell, Dan, I ain't had a good idea in eight, nine years. But it's the only thing I can think of at the moment, so I figure we might as well give it a try."

10

CLAY RIDDLE LED THE WAY out the back. There was a porch behind the house, not nearly so grand, and instead of offering a sweeping view of the valley like the front porch, it was shaded by a stand of tall cottonwoods. Brady followed the rancher down the wooden steps and onto a lawn that was patchy and well worn. There was a hitching post beside the porch, and the traffic of shod hooves had carved a path across the grass and left a few divots lying in the shade.

"How many men do you have, Mr. Riddle?" Brady asked.

"Oh, hell, Dan, I don't even know, for sure. Sometimes forty or so, sometimes half that. Hard to find good men, and harder still to keep 'em. Seems like the best ones like to move on every few months. I don't know but maybe whatever it is that makes a man a good ranch hand is the same thing that makes him a bit of a drifter."

"Cody Fallon a good hand?"

Riddle nodded, turned his head, and stopped walking. "One of the best I ever had. I'd trust that boy with my children's lives and everything I owned. That's why it's kind of hard to believe he done what he's accused of. Course, I saw him there on the floor with my own two eyes. But I still . . ." he trailed off, shaking his head as if the question were too hard for him. "If you was to ask me if he shot Wes Fraser, I'd say no way in hell. But I reckon that's why we have trials, ain't it?" Riddle added.

"I wish none of this had happened," Brady said.

"You ain't the only one, Dan. I'll tell you that. Wes Fraser was a good man. I knew him a long time. He come here just a year, maybe two, after I did. There wasn't no store when I set down my roots. But it sure made a difference havin' Wes's store, 'stead of havin' to ride fifty or sixty miles to Phillipsburg for supplies."

Riddle gnawed on his cigar. It still wasn't lit, and he took it out of his mouth, looked at the soggy end, bit it off, and stuck the shortened corona back into his mouth. He fished a match from his shirt pocket, lifted a foot to strike the match on the heel, then sucked noisily until the cigar finally took the light. He blew a couple of smoke rings, and Brady's nose tickled as the smoke wreathed around him.

Finally, satisfied that the cigar would continue to burn, Riddle turned back toward the bunkhouse, just visible through the cottonwoods. A footpath carved in the grass led to an opening among the trees, and Riddle stared at it as he walked. He appeared to be deep in thought, and Brady was reluctant to disturb him.

When the two men passed through the cottonwoods, Brady saw a couple of hands straddling a bench, with a deck of cards between them. The man facing them waved, and his opponent turned to see who had arrived. He smiled and nodded. "Howdy, Mr. Riddle," he said.

"Boys," Riddle answered, waving. "You best watch him, Foley. You're new around here, and that man settin' across from you is a bit of a cardsharp. Bottomed my pockets more than once, he has."

Foley grinned, laid two cards on the bench, and said, "I play a mean hand of poker, too, Mr. Riddle. Take more than Ray Dunhill to find the bottom of my pockets."

"I hope so, Tim," Riddle answered.

Brady watched the exchange in silence, wondering how far Clay Riddle would be willing to go to keep the easy rapport he seemed to have with his hands. A ranch the size of the Rolling R was a complex thing. Success depended as much on the relationship between rancher and hands as it did on the qualities of the rancher himself. They needed to work together, to trust one another, and, most of all, to feel as if they were all on the same side. If Clay Riddle were to testify against his own man, that trust, always fragile at best, could be shattered. That Riddle was a decent man, respected by his men, and known to be a square shooter might make a difference, but Dan Brady didn't want to count on it.

"Don Gallup around, Tim?" Riddle asked.

Foley cocked his head toward the bunkhouse wall. "Inside, I think, Mr. Riddle. Want me to get him?"

Riddle shook his head. "Naw, I'll fetch him myself."

He stepped to the bunkhouse door, which was open against the heat, and poked his head inside. "Donny," he called, "come on out here, and bring Jimmy with you, would you?"

Brady heard a muffled reply, and Riddle yanked his head back. "They'll be right out," the rancher said.

Brady felt himself tense up and was aware of the absence of weight on his hip. He felt naked now, defenseless, and he was getting skittish.

He turned his back to the bunkhouse and steeled himself. He heard footsteps, then the bang of a door. "Mr. Riddle, what's . . . what the fuck is *he* doing here?"

Without turning, Brady knew the pronoun referred to him. He turned then, feeling his fists ball in spite of his resolve to remain calm.

Gallup was scowling at him, his jaws working overtime on a wad of tobacco tucked into one cheek. Anderson stood behind him, his face neutral, his eyes never quite making contact with Brady's.

"Let's take a little walk, boys," Riddle said. His voice was hard-edged, making it plain he would brook no nonsense.

Brady watched Gallup and saw the cowboy's jawline thicken with muscle. The hand's eyes, flat and empty, flicked over Brady once, then again, but he said nothing, bowed his head for a second, and started to move, almost as if he were falling forward rather than walking.

Riddle grabbed him by the arm. "Donny, I don't want none of your bullshit, now, you understand me?"

Without waiting for an answer, the rancher took the lead, walked away from the bunkhouse with a determined stride, his heels gouging the dirt and leaving a series of small craters to mark his path. Anderson kept his eyes averted, watching the sky as he walked, his forehead beaded now with sweat. Gallup kept turning his head to look at Brady, his lips almost white, but he still held his tongue.

Riddle was leading them toward the creek, his pace quickening as he started downhill. Not until he reached a stand of cottonwoods did he say another word. When he did, his voice popped like a bullwhip. "Donny, I understand you and Jimmy saw fit to pay a visit to Mr. Brady, here, that right?"

Gallup didn't answer immediately, and Riddle was in no mood to wait. "Now, before you say anything, let me tell you exactly how things stand, just so there's no mistake. Mr. Brady is going to testify at Cody's hearing. So am I. We're going to tell the judge exactly what we saw, no more and no less. What happens then is up to the judge. But we got to do our part. I know Cody's a friend of yours, and you don't want to see him get in trouble, especially if he don't deserve it, but if he *does* get in trouble, it won't be Dan Brady's fault and it won't be mine. You understand that?"

Gallup scraped the toe of one boot on the tall grass, as if he were trying to dislodge something noxious he'd stepped in. But he still didn't say anything. He kept his eyes fixed on Brady's face, and the muscles along his jawline stood out like ropes now.

"I asked you a question, boy," Riddle snapped. "You gonna answer it, or what?"

Gallup nodded. "I understand."

"You stay away from Dan Brady's place. You

leave him alone and you by God better not go botherin' Molly Brady and her kids, or you'll answer to me. Are we clear on that?"

"Yes, sir. We're clear, all right."

"Now, I'm gonna ask you a question, and you think about it before you answer. I don't believe Cody Fallon killed Wes Fraser, but right now he's the only logical candidate. Dan says you were there before it happened and you were arguin' with Wes. Is that right?"

Gallup looked quickly at Anderson, almost as if he were expecting his friend to answer the question, and when Anderson remained silent, Gallup seemed to relax a bit. "Sort of," he said. "I mean, we had a disagreement, sort of, but it wasn't nothing."

"And you didn't see what happened?"

Gallup shook his head. "No, sir, I didn't see nothing at all."

"Jimmy," Riddle said, turning his attention to the second hand, "that right?"

"Yes sir, that's right," Anderson croaked. His voice cracked, and he had to swallow hard after he answered. There was a long silence, then Anderson's tongue slid across his lower lip with the dry, rasping sound of an old man's finger on a piece of parchment.

"All right, then, you go on back to the bunkhouse, both of you. But you remember what

I said. I hear you been bothering Dan or his family, you'll get cut loose so quick you'll think you
was hit by lightning."

Riddle watched them go, neither one turning
back. As near as Brady could tell, they said nothing to one another until they disappeared into the
bunkhouse. Riddle clapped his hands with a certain satisfaction, but the look on his face was less
confident. "I don't know whether that put the fear
of God into 'em or not, Dan, but you let me know
if they bother you again. I won't stand for it."

"I appreciate it, Clay."

"I wish to Christ I knew what really happened.
I don't like coming down on a man for something
he ain't done. But Wes Fraser's dead, and if Cody
Fallon don't know what happened, then just
maybe them two do."

"Be all over in a couple of days, I think," Brady
said. "Soon as the judge gets here, we can get on
with it."

"I hope you're right. One thing troubles me,
though."

"What's that?"

"If they don't know what happened, how can
they be so damn sure you might? Seems to me like
they're worried because they was there and because they know you were, too."

"Maybe. But maybe they're just doing the best
they know how to help out a friend."

"Cody's a good boy. I had to choose between the three of 'em who likely shot Wes, I'd pick Gallup. Nasty drunk, and from what I hear he had a snootful that day. Course, that ain't enough to convict a man. But it sure as hell is enough to make a man wonder."

Riddle's cigar had gone out again, and he jerked it out of his mouth, glared at the soggy end, then tossed it away in disgust. "Mary Jane wants me to quit smokin' those damn things. Sometimes I think maybe she's right."

"Thanks again, Clay," Brady said. "I guess I'll head on home."

"Come up for a drink first?"

"No, I don't think so. I'd better get on back."

"I reckon I'll see you at the hearing, if not before."

Brady waved goodbye and headed around the bottom of the hill. Riddle waited among the trees, chewing thoughtfully at his lower lip until Brady was out of sight, then climbed back up the hill to the house.

He was on the front porch when Brady reached his horse and waved a hand. Brady saw him fish in his pocket for something, then saw the curl of smoke as the rancher tried another cigar. Climbing into the saddle, Brady took a deep breath. He wanted to think he had solved his problem, or at least bought himself some time, but as he jerked the reins to wheel the chestnut, he felt a tingling up his spine, like a cold wind had kicked up out of nowhere. He shivered it away and started home, glancing back at the house once when he reached the bridge across the creek. Clay Riddle was still on the porch and raised a hand. At that distance, the gesture was barely visible, but Brady returned it, then squeezed the chestnut into a trot.

The sun was starting to go down now, and the sunset he'd expected looked like it was going to be spectacular. But as pretty as it was, he couldn't really keep his mind on it. There were a few too many distractions competing for his attention.

He was still three miles from home when he stopped at a shallow brook to let the horse drink. Dismounting, Brady sat in the grass at the brookside, tapping his thigh with a fistful of long grass. He saw the horse give a start, and leaned forward in time to see something slither away from the brook into the grass.

On hands and knees, he moved toward the spot, thinking maybe he'd found the answer to Kathleen's problem. There was no doubt in his mind it was a snake, but not knowing what kind, he fished a three-foot stick, its bark peeling and the soft wood underneath discolored by immersion, out of the water, and parted grass.

He saw it trapped between him and the horse in a patch of short grass. It was a garter snake, a small one, and Brady grinned like an idiot as he tried to pin the elusive thing down with the blunt end of his stick. It was gray-green, with an orange line down the center of its back, and he figured it for a black-headed garter snake. At the moment, it was only sixteen or eighteen inches long. It would reach four feet or so, but Molly didn't have to know that.

Gently, using just enough pressure to pin the snake down, he pressed the stick across the middle of its back, grabbed it behind the head, and picked it up. The frightened serpent wriggled furiously for a moment, then chose to hang limply, perhaps thinking Brady would toss it away.

Instead, he carried it to his horse, keeping it out of the chestnut's line of sight, and slipped it into his saddlebag, then swung into the saddle. Kathleen would be thrilled. Now, at least, he had something to look forward to.

11

JUDGE MITCHELL HARRISON was a man of enormous girth and an arrogance nearly as expansive. He cultivated English manners, dressed like a preacher, drank like a fish, and cussed like a gambler. His approach to the law was best characterized as flexible. In a country where the line between pragmatism and corruption seemed anything but straight, Judge Harrison managed to walk it with apparent ease, often dispensing judgment with the flowery rhetoric of Solomon via King James. He had as many admirers as he had detractors, and more than one man had found himself with a foot in both camps, depending on whose ox had been gored.

Dan Brady knew the judge by reputation only, and it was with a certain amount of trepidation that he took his seat in the first row of chairs

arranged across the front of Frank Morgan's saloon, one of the few rooms in Nogales large
enough to accommodate the witnesses, defendants,
and plaintiffs that had accumulated since Judge
Harrison's last trip through.

Harrison stood in one corner, a glass of whiskey
in his hand despite the early hour, chatting with
Matt Lowry. There were a few minor civil matters
to be dealt with, and Harrison wanted all the details so he would have at least a nodding acquaintance with the docket before he took his seat
behind the scarred wooden table that would serve
as his bench. The judge had already arranged his
gavel, a gnarled walnut mallet that gleamed with a
fresh coat of lemon oil, his Bible, to which he fre-
quently referred before passing judgment, and his
black bowler, all in a neat row across the front of
the table.

The pearl-handled Colt he always carried was
still on his hip. He had been known to use it more
than once, and his reputation had been made by
the gun a half-dozen years before, when he shot a
convicted cattle rustler as the unfortunate man
made a break for the front door after being sen-
tenced to hang. Harrison had not even bothered to
get up from behind the table on that occasion,
merely reached for the pistol and squeezed the
trigger. Some eyewitnesses to the incident swore
that he hadn't even picked the gun up off the table,

but simply let it lay there, aimed, and squeezed. Brady doubted that one, but since he hadn't been there, had to allow as how it was possible, if unlikely. The story also included the rather nice detail that Harrison, since he had saved the town the cost of a rope and a hangman, had submitted a bill for the executioner's customary fee of ten dollars, and threatened to sue when the town refused to pay.

So it was a man considerably larger than his two hundred and fifty pounds who finally pulled the Colt from his holster, set it on the table, and hammered the buzz of voices into silence with his gavel.

Harrison had a sense of theater, and took the petty disputes first. The first case concerned neighbors who had come to blows over who controlled the water rights to a creek that crossed both their properties at various points and in one place formed the border between them. The plaintiff claimed that the defendant had unlawfully diverted the stream from its bed, depriving him of fair access to the water. Harrison decided for the plaintiff on the grounds that water came from heaven and therefore belonged to all men equally, ordered the creek be restored to its natural bed, and threatened the culprit in the diversion with a substantial fine if the creek was not flowing where it should be by the time he left town.

In rapid succession, the judge dealt with a disputed land claim, the purchase of a horse that had died before the ink on the bill of sale was dry, and a mortgage foreclosure. In each case, Harrison listened impatiently to the testimony, asking questions with a certain razor edge, as if he were annoyed at everybody in the room for taking up his time. Brady wondered whether Harrison were anxious to get to Cody Fallon, since capital crimes gave him that most exalted platform from which to declaim.

All during the civil cases, Brady kept watching the young cowboy. Fallon seemed confused, even dazed, if not by his surroundings then by his unexpected presence at the center of the day's biggest attraction. His eyes kept darting from judge to witness stand and back. He was hanging on every word, as if trying to gather enough information about Harrison and his thought processes to divine his own fate.

Brady knew, as did everyone else in the courtroom, that Harrison reserved his harshest sentences for such crimes, and if he decided Fallon ought to be brought to trial, then the young cowboy was already halfway to the gallows. But Harrison was rigorous in his adherence to the law and its underlying logic. He prided himself on seeing things that others couldn't see and demanding answers to questions no one else ever thought to ask.

Harrison pounded his gavel, looked at Matt

Lowry, and smiled a cold smile. It tugged his beard like an invisible hand, and his eyes were cold and flat when he looked at the assembly. "Sheriff, I believe we're ready for the real business of the day," he said. "You ready?"

"Yes, your honor, I'm ready."

"Good, why don't you raise your right hand then, and we'll swear you in?"

Lowry faced the makeshift bench, let his left hand rest on the well-worn leather of Harrison's Bible, and promised to tell the truth as he knew it. Harrison nodded, with just the slightest bow of his head, and just once. "Let me hear," he said.

Lowry ran through the details, sketching them carefully but trying to avoid being long-winded. When he was done, Harrison excused him, saying, "Let's hear from the accused before I ask you a few questions, Matt, shall we?"

Lowry got up from the witness chair and took a seat next to Brady. He leaned over and whispered, "He's in a bad mood today. I don't know whether that's bad for us or bad for Cody Fallon."

Brady was about to respond when he saw Harrison scowling at him, and nudged Lowry with his elbow.

From the corner of his mouth, Lowry whispered, "See what I mean?"

Cody Fallon took the oath, then sat in the chair, his long legs bent double under the low chair. He perched on the front edge of the seat, as if not sure he wanted to sit at all, and kept fidgeting with his hands, tugging at his collar, and twisting his head from side to side, trying to loosen the tension that danced under his skin like frightened mice.

"Mr. Fallon, you heard what Matt said, did you?" Harrison asked.

"Yes, sir, your honor, I did."

"And what do you have to say for yourself?"

"I didn't do it, your honor. I didn't shoot Mr. Fraser. I never shot a man in my whole life."

"Weren't in the war, then, were you?" Harrison asked.

"Oh, yes, sir, I was. But I was in the Quartermaster Corps. Never did get to carry a gun."

"You don't deny that you were there when Mr. Fraser got shot, do you?"

"I must have been, sir. I mean, he was okay when I saw him last."

"You were unconscious when the sheriff found you, is that right?"

"I guess so, your honor. I mean, when I come to, Wes . . . Mr. Fraser . . . had already been shot. He was lying there on the floor, but I didn't hardly know where I was, let alone what happened."

"How did you come to be unconscious?"

"Well, like I told the sheriff, I had had a few drinks, and I slipped on something on the floor. I remember falling, and I remember hitting my head, my face, actually, on the edge of the counter in Mr. Fraser's store. It's got a metal edge on it, and it's pretty hard wood, so that's the last thing I remember."

"So you didn't see the shooting?"

"No, sir."

"And you don't know who did it, is that right?"

"No, sir, I don't."

Harrison cleared his throat and leaned back in his chair. He bobbed his head, almost as if he were in a rocker, but the rest of his body stayed motionless. He looked at the sheriff. "Matt," he said, "let me ask you a few questions. Remember you're still under oath."

"Yes, sir." Lowry started to get up, but Harrison waved him back into his chair. "You might as well stay there. We'll keep Mr. Fallon up here where I can watch him close. He say anything different from what you remember?"

"No, your honor. He didn't say much now and he didn't say much then, either."

"You say you have a couple of witnesses, too, that right?"

"Yes, sir, three."

"Well, let's hear what they have to say. Get 'em up here, Matt. It's been a long morning."

Lowry touched Brady on the shoulder, gave it a squeeze, and half pushed him toward the bench. Brady, without being asked, placed his hand on the Bible, and swore himself in.

"State your name," Harrison said, cocking his head to one side and peering at Brady with a skeptical expression, as if he expected him to lie.

"Daniel Brady."

"You saw the shooting?"

"No, sir. I heard it."

"You heard it."

"Yes, sir. I had been in the store, Wes Fraser's store. But I was outside when the shooting occurred."

Harrison stuck the surprisingly delicate tip of his tongue between his lips, traced the contours of his mouth, then reached up to smooth his beard with his left hand. "But you didn't see it happen?"

"No, sir, I didn't."

"But you know that Mr. Fallon, here, did the shooting, is that right?"

"No, sir, I don't know that for a fact. I know he and two other men were in the store just before the shooting. But I . . ."

"Two other men, you say?"

Harrison looked at Lowry. "Matt, these two men, they your other two witnesses?"

"No, sir, they're not."

Speaking as if Brady weren't even there, Harrison said, "I hope they have more to say than this Brady feller." The judge looked at Brady again, leaned back a little in his chair, and said, "Suppose you tell me everything in your own words. If I have any questions, I'll interrupt you. How would that be?"

"Fine, sir." Brady hesitated a moment, then launched into his story. He kept his eyes fixed on Harrison, trying to guess what the judge was thinking, but it didn't take a mind-reader to see that the judge was less than impressed with Brady's story. When he was finished, he looked at Cody Fallon, who was still sitting in the witness chair, his head bowed, his hands folded between his legs as if he was trying to keep them warm.

"So, let me see if I can sum it all up, Mr. Brady, how would that be?"

"Whatever you say, Judge."

"All right, then. You were witness to an argument between Mr. Fraser and three men, one of whom is the accused. You had some words with two of the men yourself, but Mr. Fallon assured you there was nothing to worry about, and Mr. Fraser did not seem concerned, as if he was used to arguing with these fellows. You went outside, went to another store, and when you came back to your wagon, you heard a gunshot. You went to fetch the sheriff while two other men watched the store. That about it?"

Brady, realizing just how little he had really seen, nodded weakly. "That's about it, your honor."

"So, you didn't see the other two men leave the store. In fact, you didn't see them at all, or anybody else, for that matter, once you heard the gunshot. Is that right?"

Brady nodded. "That's right."

"You heard glass break, and it turns out that it was probably, and I emphasize that, probably the window to the back door of the store. But as far as you know, anyone could have done the shooting."

"I guess that's right, your honor."

"You do, do you? You guess so?"

Brady shrugged. Reduced to its essence, there was so little to his testimony, he sensed that he had been right all along, there was no point in giving it at all. No matter what he believed, what he could honestly state was paltry indeed.

"All right, let me hear what the other two witnesses have to say, and I'll see if I need to ask you anything else. Remember that you're still under oath."

Clay Riddle went next, told how he had been getting a shave. He hadn't heard the gunshot and hadn't seen anyone leave Fraser's store. He explained how they had discovered Fallon unconscious and found the back door had been broken, presumably allowing someone to escape out the back way.

Al Fisher, looking peculiar without his white smock, his gray hair tangled where he kept running his fingers through it, had even less to say.

When Fisher finished, Harrison hummed to himself, something that sounded vaguely like "Rock of Ages" but Brady couldn't be sure. The judge looked at Matt Lowry. "What about them other two fellers, sheriff, the ones who were in the dead man's store with the accused? They here?"

"They didn't see anything, Judge. They claim they left the store before anything happened."

"And you believe them?"

"I don't know whether to believe them or not, Judge. But they say they weren't there when it happened, and I can't prove they were. The only man who could was Wes Fraser himself, if Fallon's telling the truth."

Harrison tapped one foot restlessly on the floor under the table. Brady watched the rising and falling of the highly polished boot without hearing it. All he could hear was the beating of his own heart. He knew what was going to happen, and part of him was relieved. He felt bad that whoever had shot Wes Fraser was going to get away with it, but he'd done everything he could. It was up to the judge, and he knew what he'd do if he were making the decision.

And Harrison wasted no time. "Matt, seems to me like I got no choice but to let Mr. Fallon go. I didn't hear anything to make me think he'd be convicted of anything but being a clumsy fool. I think a trial would be a waste of time." He closed his thick fingers around the handle of the gavel, rapped it sharply, and said, "Case dismissed."

Cody Fallon continued to sit there, his head still bowed, and Lowry had to shake him to get his attention. "You can go, Cody," he said.

Fallon nodded dumbly. His eyes were glazed, fixed on someplace a thousand miles beyond Matt Lowry's head. "All right," he said.

Harrison got to his feet, leaned toward Fallon, and said, "You remember anything else, young feller, you be sure and let Matt know. It don't set right with me what happened here, but right now there ain't a damn thing can be done about it."

Fallon nodded again.

The makeshift courtroom was already empty of everyone except Brady, Fallon, the sheriff, and the judge. Brady looked around at the room, now seeming so huge. He felt empty inside, even emptier than the room, feeling as if he had somehow failed Wes Fraser, that if he had done something different, he might have saved him, or at least seen to it that whoever shot him paid a price for it.

But now that the law had had its say, there was nothing more to be done.

12

BRADY WALKED TOWARD the door and on through, turning only when he was out on the boardwalk. Cody Fallon was still sitting in the witness chair, his face averted from the judge and Sheriff Lowry, who stood beside him, talking softly. Brady hoped to catch Fallon's eye, but the young cowhand never looked up. For a moment, Brady wanted to go back inside, tell him no hard feelings, that he only did what he thought was right, but he doubted that Fallon would care, and even wondered whether the kid was capable of understanding anything at the moment.

He backed away from the door, feeling the sun on his back. It was nearly noon, and he was hungry. And, more than food, he needed a drink, something strong that would slide down easy, then explode in his belly, flood his body with warmth to kill the chill deep inside him, and steady his nerves. He stepped off the boardwalk and started up the street toward Sam Chatmon's Saloon.

He was halfway there when he heard someone hailing him. Turning to look back, he saw Matt Lowry waving at him, then heard the sheriff holler for him to wait. He turned all the way around and stood in the street, only dimly aware of his surroundings.

Lowry broke into a bandy-legged sprint, his short legs pumping and his gunbelt flapping on his hip like the wing of an injured bird. When the sheriff caught up to him, he draped an arm over Brady's shoulder. "Come on, Dan, I'll buy you a drink," he said.

"I don't know if . . ."

"The hell with that. You need one and so do I." Without waiting for an argument, he started to tug Brady toward the saloon, keeping a firm grip on Brady's upper arm, a grip more appropriate to apprehending a felon than coaxing a friend into a saloon, but Brady ignored the pressure.

Once inside, Lowry grabbed a table, pushed Brady into a chair, and went over to the bar, glancing back to make certain Brady didn't try to leave. The place stank of sour beer and damp sawdust that clotted on the soles of his boots. The dark wood and high ceiling gave Chatmon's a cavelike atmosphere, and in the shadows among the rafters,

Brady suspected bats would have found a comfortable home. Bright sunlight splattered on the grimy front window, but not much made it through the glass, and the place was cool and damp.

A couple of dozen cowhands, most of them from the Rolling R, had bellied up to the bar or clustered around tables. Three men were playing billiards, their hats pushed back on their foreheads to give them a clear sight line along their cues, and the clink of the balls punctuated the low hum of a half-dozen conversations. Clay Riddle was at the bar, and when he saw Lowry, he went over to him, then turned, saw Dan, and came over to the table.

"You all right, Dan?" he asked.

Brady nodded. "Yeah, I'm fine, Clay."

The rancher shrugged as if in response to a question Brady hadn't asked, then hunched his shoulders like a man trying to keep warm. "I guess things can get back to normal around here, now," he said.

"I suppose so."

"Try to put it behind you, Dan. You did what you could."

"I hope Sarah Fraser can do that."

At the mention of Wes Fraser's widow, Riddle's face seemed to shrink, as if collapsing in on itself, and the knit brows gathered shadows in their furrows, darkening the whole appearance of the rancher, as if a storm cloud had suddenly begun to swirl around him.

Shaking his head, he said, "I feel real bad about Sarah. A few of us are taking up a collection, see if we can get enough together to tide her over until she decides what she wants to do. Right now, she's thinking about selling the store and going back East. I guess that's the best thing."

Lowry was back, a pair of shot glasses in one hand, a pair of beers in the other. He set the four glasses on the table, dropped into a chair, and said, "Feel free to join us, Clay."

Riddle shook his head. "No, thanks, Matt. I got to get back to work." He touched the brim of his hat and headed for the door, stopping briefly at his table to chat with Pete Allen, his foreman.

When Riddle was gone, Lowry reached out with an extended finger, nudged one of the shot glasses toward Brady, and said, "Bottoms up, Dan. It'll do you good."

Brady picked up the glass, held it high to catch the light, and swirled the whiskey around for a moment, then downed it in a single swallow. He felt the familiar heat as the whiskey bottomed out, and set the glass on the table. He reached for the beer, curled both hands around the glass, but left it on the table.

"Anything wrong, Dan?" Lowry asked.

Brady looked at him. "Hell, I don't know, Matt. Maybe nothing, maybe everything."

"Look, I know you feel bad about Wes. We all do. And it don't seem right that whoever shot him got off scot-free, but what can we do?"

Brady bobbed his head and, for a moment, he thought it would never stop, like his skull sat on a spring and would rock back and forth forever. He felt a little giddy, but it wasn't relief that tingled through his nerves. He felt like things were out of control, as if things all around him were happening no matter what he wanted, and there wasn't a thing he could do about any of them.

He took a sip of the beer, lowered the glass carefully to the table, and curled his hands around it once again. "Matt," he said, "you and I both know that it was probably Gallup and Anderson who shot Wes. Maybe Fallon was part of it, and maybe he wasn't. Maybe he even tried to stop it, but we know what happened, and there's nothing we can do about it. It doesn't seem right, somehow."

"That's a bad thing, Dan. I know that. I mean, if there was anything I could do, don't you think I'd do it? But we can't prove Gallup done anything. We can't even prove he was there, let alone that he pulled the trigger. What do you want me to do, lock him up and starve him into confessing?"

"Why did Gallup threaten me, do you think? I mean, if he isn't guilty?"

"I don't know, maybe he was just trying to stick

up for his friend. Maybe he figured we'd be so anxious to get somebody we'd get Fallon. It could be that simple, you know."

"Yeah, it could, but I don't believe it."

"Dan, I don't want you doing anything stupid. You let things be a while. I'll keep my eyes open, maybe I'll get lucky. If that happens, then maybe . . ."

"You talk like you expect Gallup to admit it."

"No, of course not. But he likes his liquor. And when he gets to drinkin', he gets to talkin'. Maybe he'll make a mistake, maybe Anderson will crack. Maybe Fallon will remember something. You never know what could happen."

"They're all in it together. They'll look out for one another."

"Let it go, Dan. There's nothing you can do. You can't keep thinking about it, brooding on it. It'll fester, and it'll eat you up."

Brady shook his head. "No, it won't eat me up, Matt. But I won't forget about it, either. I can't. Don Gallup threatened me, and he did that for some reason. And I'll tell you one thing right now. He comes near my place again, I'll kill him, sure as I'm sitting here."

"No you won't either. I won't allow it. If he threatens you, defend yourself, but don't go looking for trouble. I can't sit back and let this become a feud, Dan. It's got to stop. The law will handle it."

"I saw the law at work this morning, Matt. The law can't do anything, and you and I both know that."

"What do you want, you want me to hang Fallon without a trial? Is that what you want? You want to settle this by Brady's law? Or Lowry's?"

"No. Of course not."

"Well, you were there, you heard the testimony. Hell, you said yourself you didn't see what happened. How in hell could you expect Mitch Harrison to do anything but what he done? Look, I admire what you did. I respect the fact that you stood up, even though I know it cost you something. But what's done is done. Unless something else happens, it's ancient history, Dan, dead and buried."

Remembering he'd told himself the same thing not twenty minutes before, Brady grunted. "Yeah," he said, "dead and buried. Just like Wes Fraser."

"That's uncalled for."

"Well, it's true, isn't it?"

"Yeah," Lowry said. "It's true. But . . ."

"I feel so . . . I can't explain it. But I feel like I did something wrong. Like it's my fault Wes is dead. You know what that's like, Matt?"

"Damn right I do. It comes with the badge, Dan. I see all kinds of things I know ain't right, but some of them I can't do a damn thing about. And when

I can do something, it don't make me feel any better about those times when I can't. Look, you did all you could. So did Clay Riddle and Al Fisher. But you can't take it personal. You just can't. You got to let the law take its course. And if the law don't work, then you spit in the street and walk away, because if you don't, then you're taking the law into your own hands. Is that what you want? You want Brady's law because the one we got don't work a hundred percent?"

"What I want is to live my life. I want to be left alone. I want to sit on the porch and watch my kids grow up. I want to take long walks in the hills with Molly without having to carry a gun or look over my shoulder every fifty yards because Don Gallup might be out there, or Cody Fallon."

"I'm proud of what you did this morning. Mitch Harrison told me to tell you that it took a lot of courage to do what you done, and I agree with him. But you don't have to worry about them fellers bothering you now. If they think about it at all, even if they are guilty, they'll see that bothering you is just ripping a scab off something that ought to be let heal. Why would they risk it? Why would they want to call attention to themselves, get themselves in more hot water? Hell, they just climbed out of the pot, why crawl back in?"

Brady didn't answer right away. Instead, he

watched the bubbles in his beer, tiny wavering columns like miniature jewels floating toward the surface. He hoisted the glass and took a long pull, wiping the foam from his upper lip with a fingertip. He stood up. "I guess maybe you're right, Matt," he said.

"Sure I am. Put it behind you, Dan. Get on with your life."

Brady tried to smile, but it felt brittle on his lips, and his cheeks didn't want to flex at all. He waved, leaned over to snatch at the glass, and drained off the last of the beer. "Thanks for the drink," he said. "See you in a couple of days."

"How you gettin' on with that new barn?"

"Almost done. But I'll tell you, when it finally is finished, I don't want to look at another goddamned nail for the rest of my life."

Lowry laughed. "Hell, soon as I retire, I'll be building myself a barn, and I kinda hoped you'd pitch in, seein' how you have all this experience, and all."

"The first day a snowball don't melt in hell, I'll be over with my hammer," Brady said.

He walked outside. The street was strangely quiet. The only sound was the swish of horse tails and the buzz of flies around the fresh horse apples in the dirt. Matt Lowry was right, and Brady knew it, but he wondered whether Molly would be as certain. With her distaste for Nogales, it wasn't likely she'd be any too happy. But he was too damned old to start over. He would just have to hope that she could learn to accept it. In a few months, it would be ancient history, like Matt Lowry had said.

13

AS SOON AS HE GOT HOME, Brady broke the news to Molly. She seemed to take it well, nodding her head now and then as he described the hearing. She asked no questions until he was done, and then asked only, "What do we do now?"

It was the one question that had monopolized Brady's attention on the long ride, and still he had no answer. But he knew he couldn't leave it there between them like a vacuum that could suck their entire lives into it, and he said, "We go on as we have always done. I've got a barn to finish, a fence to finish. We have two children to raise, and I'll be damned if something like this is going to get in the way."

"You don't think maybe we should move away?"

He shook his head. He knew it was partly pride

and partly stubbornness, but there was no way he was going to give in to the impulse to flee. "Why should we?" he asked. "I did what I had to do, and that's the end of it. As far as I'm concerned, it's over. Life goes on."

"You don't think those men will come back?"

"No. Why should they? I don't know whether they did anything, whether they killed Wes Fraser or not, but there's no reason for them to bother us again."

"Even if the sheriff is still trying to find out what happened?"

Brady took a long breath. "Yes," he said, "even if Matt is still looking for the killers."

"You think they did it, though, don't you? You think those men murdered Mr. Fraser, don't you?"

"I don't know, Moll." He looked at her intently, half expecting her to challenge his answer, but it was the truth. He didn't know. He knew only what he thought, but he was not certain, not certain enough, at any rate. In his gut, he knew, all right, knew for sure that Gallup and Anderson, and maybe Cody Fallon, were guilty. But his brain was less certain, maybe less reliable, too, but surely less certain.

She nodded then, but whether from agreement or resignation, he couldn't tell. "All right, I guess."

He didn't bother to eat lunch, just went out to the barn, strapped on the apron, and started to work. He had two walls to go, and he wanted to get the barn finished by the end of the week. It was hot and he worked up a sweat in a real hurry. His shoulders began to ache from the hammering. He drove the nails like a man in a frenzy, only half conscious of the furious assault that rattled his bones. It seemed at times that he was trying to tear something down rather than build something, and twice he split boards by giving a nailhead one additional, unnecessary blow.

Kathleen came into the barn at one point, a grasshopper in her hands, and he watched silently as she went to the wooden box he'd made for her snake. She lifted the screen, dropped the grasshopper in, and jumped with a squeal, clapping her hands together. She looked at him almost as if she were apologizing for interrupting him, but when he smiled, she seemed to relax, and replaced the screen.

"Did he eat the grasshopper, Kath?" Brady asked.

"I don't know."

"We'll have to ask around, ask somebody who knows what garter snakes like to eat."

She nodded. "All right."

"Suppose he likes to eat mice?"

"Ugh!"

Brady laughed, watched her walk back to the house, still shaking her head at the horrid thought, then turned back to his work. Watching his daughter had reminded him why he was working. But his anger was driving him, and he worked more quickly than he could ever remember working. By late afternoon, he had one wall finished, and stood back to look at his handiwork. Backing away, he canted his head to one side, eyed the alignment, and when it passed muster, walked to the house, leaving the tool apron around his waist. With every step, he clattered as if he were draped in sleighbells, the random music of clinking nails and rattling tools somehow soothing, as if it celebrated a return to normalcy.

He was tired, but determined to keep going until it got too dark to see. Molly was inside, working on the curtains, a thimble gleaming on one thumb as she basted a hem, her long fingers amazingly graceful as she worked the needle with precision that was almost mechanical. She looked up as he stepped in. "I heard you coming," she said, smiling for what seemed to Dan the first time in months.

He looked at the apron, patted it, and sent another tinkling crescendo echoing around the room. "Needed a break," he said.

"You must be exhausted. You've been hammering like a madman."

"It feels good to get back to normal," he said, dropping into a chair, taking care not to bang the table with his tools. "With any luck, I'll have the walls up by sundown tomorrow."

"I'll help you paint it, when you're ready," she said. "You hungry?"

He nodded.

"I'll get you something to eat as soon as I finish this hem." The needle flashed in a band of sunlight spilling through the curtainless window, the thread whispering as she tugged it through after each stroke. The final foot seemed to take no time at all, and Molly stood up, carefully folding her work before setting it on her chair, the needle and spool of thread resting in the slight hollow made by their weight.

Molly and the children had already eaten, and Brady wolfed down his food, anxious to get back to work while the light held. When he was finished, Molly walked him out to the barn, standing by while he stopped at the well for a dipperful of cold water. He pumped a pail full, filled a dipper, and took one long gulping draft. He refilled the dipper from the pail and poured it over his head, enjoying the feel of the cool water as it soaked his shirt and ran in rivulets under the drenched cotton.

When they reached the barn, Molly stood behind him, her hands on his shoulders, kneading the knots of taut muscle over his collarbones. "You sure you want to work anymore today, hon?" she asked. She let her head rest on his shoulder, and he reached back to stroke her hair, then turned to kiss her on the crown of her head, burying his nose in the fragrant curls.

"What I'd like is never to work again, Moll, but since that's out of the question, I guess I might as well finish. My father used to say that a man only had so much work in his life. Maybe if I get mine done early, I'll have some time to sit in a rocker before I die."

"Your father was trying to be an optimist. There's always something to do. You know that. So did he."

"Yeah, I guess so. But it feels good now, like the hammer is part of my arm."

"Don't overdo it, Dan, all right? No sense making yourself sick."

"I'll be fine. It'll feel good when I'm finished."

She slipped a hand inside his shirt then, ignoring the soggy cotton, and let it rest over his heart. She could feel it beating, like a small, trapped animal throbbing under her palm. Dan let his own hand rest over hers, only the sopping cloth of his shirt between them, squeezed her fingers, then extricated himself from her grasp. "Back to work," he said.

He watched Molly walk back to the house, her hair catching the sunlight so it seemed full of fire as it swung back and forth in time to her steps. Unlike most of the women in Nogales, she preferred jeans to dresses, and the snug fit of the denim over her hips made him wonder whether he ought to forget about working for the rest of the evening. But there was still too much frustration sputtering in his nerves like fire racing through dry grass and, regretfully, he watched her go inside, then turned back to his work.

As exhaustion overtook him, he settled into a more reasonable pace, but still managed to get half of the remaining wall boarded. He was working from a ladder for the higher reaches, nailing the top of several boards in place, then climbing down to nail the bottoms in. His legs ached from going up and down the ladder, and his shoulders felt as if someone had stabbed them with red-hot needles. "Enough," he whispered, then, louder, said it again, "Enough!"

Wearily, he untied the apron, let it fall to the ground with a clank, and bent over to retrieve it. The sun was just beginning to set, and he walked to the west end of the barn, sat down, and leaned back against the rough timber to watch the day die.

A hot wind swirled across the grass, catching dust here and there, small funnels like tiny tornadoes wobbling into oblivion. Far to the northwest, the mountains turned purple as brilliant orange light gushed from behind a wall of clouds. He felt cramped, and kept shifting his position to ease the pain in his tortured body. His eyes closed for a moment, and when he opened them again, the sun was gone. Only the roof of heaven was still lit, the mountains turned now to coal, the trees covering their flanks charred hulks, all but indistinguishable from shadow. Closer in, the cottonwoods along Hanley Creek shivered in the breeze, and he could hear the hiss of the wind in the grass. It looked like it might rain, and he was thankful he'd managed to get as much done as he had.

Getting to his feet, he walked to the corner of the barn, glanced briefly at the house, saw the orange rectangle of one of the windows still needing curtains, and looked back to the approaching storm. The air was still hot, but there was an undercurrent on the wind, a chill that made the sweat on his brow and his neck feel like ice.

He walked along the fence, keeping one eye on the sky. His horses seemed to sense the advancing rain, as they tossed their manes and swished their tails, nickering and pawing the ground now and then. He vaulted over the fence, feeling the explosion of fire in his knees and hips, the jolt when he landed compressing the flame into bolts of lightning that raced from joint to joint.

Behind him, he could hear Molly calling to him, "Dan? Where are you? Dan?"

Ignoring her, he lay down in the grass, felt it prickle against his exposed skin, and stretched his arms out in the long green blades the way he had in snow when a child. Making angels, they called it, and he wondered if the impress of his body would linger in the grass as long as it had in the snows of the Ohio winter. Sitting up, he got to his knees, then to his feet, backing away from the hollow in the grass. Where he had been was empty now, his presence marked by the bent and broken blades that would spring back overnight, all trace of him gone in a matter of hours.

Looking up at the sky, the last blades of sunlight spearing out in every direction from behind the clouds, he felt impossibly small, as if his very existence had been reduced to that single transitory hollow in the grass. He thought about what would happen if he were to take Molly and the kids and leave, head west, maybe back East, leaving the stillborn homestead to the ravages of time and weather. The barn would fall one day and rot, weeds would spring up among the sun-bleached ruins, eventually hiding it altogether. The fence would fall, the posts rot through and topple. The well would cave in on itself, the earth taking back its water, hiding it again. Even the house would disappear, leaving only broken panes of glass behind, small shards that would reflect the sun, gather dust, and slowly disappear sliver by sliver until all traces of Dan Brady and his family were gone.

He had worked too hard to let that happen, put

in too much of himself, taken too much from his family in the attempt to carve some temporary little niche in the wall of time, a place where they could spend what few years were allotted to them, clinging to the spinning planet like bugs on a leaf whirling in a flood. To let go was to die, to disappear, and he'd be damned if he would let go, not now. Let Don Gallup come, if he dared. He would find that Dan Brady wasn't all that easy to dislodge, to frighten, to scare off. This was his place, by God, and it meant too much to let some drunken bully make him walk away from it.

14

SLEEP WAS HARD TO COME BY. Brady lay in bed, listening to Molly breathe. She tossed and turned, her limbs warring with some demon Brady could neither see nor hear. Once, he got up and went out on the porch, slipping a heavy flannel shirt on to ward off the chill. The moon was low on the horizon, its light pale, bleaching everything to a dull gray. The cottonwoods down by the creek looked as if they had been carved from lead and coal. Even the shadows of the trees seemed wan and half-hearted, as if the moon were sucking up the darkness.

On the hillside, he could make out some of his horses, neutral smears of faint color, almost shapeless and immobile. He felt as if everything were somehow slipping away from him, as if he were watching the world from a mountaintop far away, everything below him made tiny and meaningless by the immense distance. The chill seeped into his bones, and he felt himself shivering, but he refused to go back inside. There was some strange comfort outdoors, as if some part of him he hadn't known was there wanted to be powerless, useless, impotent.

He went inside only long enough to roll a cigarette, then returned to the porch. He walked around to the back of the house, and stood beside the bedroom window. Through the narrow gap of the partially raised sash, he could hear Molly thrashing in the covers and once her voice, somewhere between a moan and a whimper. He turned to the window then and leaned close to look inside. In the moonlight, he could see her outline under the blankets, one arm wrapped around her head, the other thrown wide as if groping for him in her sleep.

Satisfied that she was all right, he turned away, scraped the match against the side of the house, lit the cigarette, and walked down to the barn. In the pale light from the moon, it looked finished, as if it had been painted gray. He walked inside, looked up at the rafters, just visible in the light spilling in through the unfinished wall. The loft was pitch-black, only its front edge clearly discernible. He felt good looking at it, proud of his handiwork, despite the aching in his body from the forced labor of the long afternoon.

Brady sucked greedily on the cigarette, blowing the smoke out in long plumes that looked like sheaves of silver filigree in the moonlight. Idly, he waved his hand through one, half expecting to feel the tingle of delicate strands wrapping themselves around his fingers.

Back outside, he finished the cigarette, stubbed it out, and walked back to the house. Despite his exhaustion, he felt confident about the morning, almost hopeful. He could finish the barn without killing himself, then he and Molly could paint it. He wanted to have both the barn and the fence ready by fall, before the weather turned cold and the snow would make further work outdoors unrealistic.

Climbing back onto the porch, he wrapped one arm around a column supporting its roof, felt the hard edge of the timber digging into his flesh, and squeezed it hard, relishing the discomfort the way a man will take pleasure from poking at an aching tooth. He sat down by the fireplace where the coals of a single log glowed dully under a layer of feathery ash. He leaned over, fanned the ashes away with his hand, and felt the warmth of the exposed embers on his skin.

There is so much here to like, he thought, so much worth working for, even fighting for. If only he could persuade Molly to feel the same way. At the thought of his wife, he got to his feet, walked to one window in the kitchen where the new curtains had already been hung. He curled his fingers around the cloth, gathering it gently and letting his hand hang there. It was soothing somehow, knowing that she had worked the cloth with her own hands, made the curtains the same way he had made the barn.

These were things that belonged to them not only because they possessed them, but because they had invested part of themselves in their making. It was a way of making a mark, creating something from nothing just to prove that you existed. That they existed together was the single most important fact of his relatively uneventful life.

Once more, he went out to the porch, as if the heat of the dying embers had been too much for him. He shivered immediately, and hugged himself as he moved to the edge of the porch. It still seemed strange to him that such hot days could be followed by nights so cool. He kept thinking about his life, its tiny details, so insignificant, so meaningless to anyone but him.

He was no hero, had made no mark in history, and never would. But that was all right with Brady. He didn't aspire to immortality, just a respectable mortality, living out his days surrounded by his family, the people who meant the most to him and for whom he lived each ordinary day.

Brady was about to go back inside when he saw

a shadow moving just below the hilltop beyond the horses, as if something was moving along the far side of the hill trying to stay out of sight. At first he thought it might be a wolf moving in on the horses, or maybe a cougar, although it would be the first he'd seen this far from the rocky foothills. He closed his eyes, then opened them again trying to focus on the blurred shadow, but it was gone, if it had been there at all. He watched for several minutes, but when he saw nothing further, decided it had been his imagination.

He went inside, thinking he would try to sleep, but the memory of that shadow was too vivid. It couldn't have been his imagination. He found his boots by the hearth and pulled them on. He reached up over the mantel and took down the Winchester. Taking off the safety, he moved to the door, feeling a little silly, as if he was overreacting, but knowing that unless he checked, he wouldn't be able to sleep anyway.

He slipped outside, moved to the corner of the house, and knelt to give himself a better angle on the hilltop. Still, he saw nothing, but that didn't mean nothing was there. He started toward the half-finished fence, vaulted over it, and sprinted across the hillside toward the clump of alders to the west. The horses were skittish now, as if they too had sensed something they couldn't see.

At a small depression in the hillside full of scrub

oak, he stopped to listen. Instinctively, he glanced back at the house, realizing that he'd left the door unlocked. There was a chance, slim but real, that it could have been Apaches. They loved to raid for horses, and ranged as far east as the Texas panhandle. He hadn't heard rumors that they were on the loose, but Victorio and his band were out there somewhere, in the New Mexican mountains, and there was no reason why they couldn't have come this way.

At the thought of Apaches, his skin prickled, and a cold sweat beaded his brow despite the chilly air. He could feel the wind moving across the hillside, see the silvered grass bending, hear it hissing. One of the horses nickered, then broke into a stiff-legged trot. Several of the others followed it down the hill. He levered a round into the chamber, trying to muffle the metallic click with spread fingers and palm.

He wished he'd paid more attention to his marksmanship, and resolved to spend a little time over the next few days practicing. He thought about his Colt, tucked away in a trunk somewhere, and decided it might not be a bad idea to dig it up, clean it, and fire a few rounds, just to get used to the feel of a pistol in his hand once more. Part of him felt as if he were playacting, a little boy confronting demons, planning to kill ghosts with bullets, while part of him whispered that it was only prudent to be prepared for anything—Apaches, cowboys, wolves, cougars—a man *had* to be ready for anything out here, and a man alone had one friend . . . his gun.

There was still no sign that anything was up there beyond the crest of the hill. He started to relax, moved away from the oak-filled hollow, and eased up the hill. He failed to notice a small slab of stone, tripped over it, and sprawled headlong uphill, the Winchester clattering on the rock as he fell.

Retrieving the gun, he cursed silently. The air had been crushed from his lungs, and he gasped for breath, trying to be quiet but feeling as if every inhalation rolled across the valley like muttering thunder. He saw a shapeless mass of shadow near the top of the hill then, and squinted, trying to resolve it into something identifiable.

He heard another nicker, but it was more distant, coming from somewhere on the other side of the hill. Then he heard the thud of hooves on the turf, and he scrambled to his feet. Racing up the steep incline, he closed on the shapeless mass, but didn't recognize it for what it was until he was within a few feet. By then, he knew that he had not been wrong. Something had been there all right, something lethal. The shadowy bulk was one of his horses. He could smell the cloying sweetness of fresh blood, and the animal wasn't moving, not at all. There wasn't a sound now, no wheezing of breath, no wind in the cottonwood leaves, nothing at all.

He knelt beside the horse for a moment, leaning close to try and see what had happened to it. For an instant, he thought about striking a match, but knew the spurt of flame could give him away if his visitors were two-legged, red or white. The moonlight faded as he leaned over the horse, and he glanced up to see a massive cloud just beginning to cover the moon. The fading light gleamed in the black stain of blood on the mare's chest, but there was no sign of tooth or claw, no indication that either a wolf or a cougar had gotten to it.

And he thought back over the past half hour, realizing that a wild animal would have spooked the horses at its first onslaught, that the horse would have made enough noise to wake the dead. Whatever had gotten to the mare had not frightened it, had gotten close enough to kill silently.

He moved around the carcass and sprinted toward the top of the hill, the Winchester suddenly seeming a frail and flimsy thing in his sweaty hands. When he reached the crest, he nearly lost his footing as the hill flattened out suddenly, and he had to break stride to recover his balance.

He heard what sounded like footsteps, saw something move out of the trees to his left, and swung the rifle in that direction. Down below, he

saw shapes moving in the brush, then the movement resolved into the figure of a running man.
Whoever it was was wearing a Stetson, and this
pushed his worry about Apaches aside.

He called out, "Stop!" But the running man ignored him, picking up his pace as he reached a
point where the slope of the hill flattened a bit and
footing was more secure. Brady raced after him in
the dark, cursing his luck, and whispering to the
moon, "Come on, dammit, come on out!"

More figures detached themselves from the
brush far below, and he could see the silhouettes of
two men on horseback, a third, riderless horse between them. He wanted to shoot, but didn't know
how many there were. He ran faster, but the fleeing figure was far ahead of him. When he reached
the gentler slope, he quickened his pace, but the
fugitive had widened the gap between them, and
was only a few yards from his companions now.

He heard a voice as one of the mounted men
called to the runner, but he didn't recognize it.
Once more, he called out to the men to stop, but
the runner slipped in between his colleagues and
swung into the saddle. It was starting to brighten a
little, but still not enough for him to see the men
clearly.

His aching joints protested with every step, and
the hammering on his knees filled them with
molten lead. The moon continued its slow reap-

pearance, and the grass all around Brady started to turn gray again. He saw something bright, fittings of a saddle, then the dull gleam of spur as the leftmost rider wheeled his mount and kicked it. The two remaining men followed suit, breaking into a trot in a ragged line against the brush.

The moon suddenly exploded into full view, flooding the valley with its light, and he saw the last man in profile, clearly enough to recognize Don Gallup. The man turned, raised a fist, and shouted something Brady couldn't understand, then lashed his horse with fisted reins. His spurs flashed, then jingled as he dug them into the horse's flank and pulled them free. The horse spurted forward gaining on the two riders ahead of him.

Dropping to one knee, Brady raised the Winchester. He was shaking with rage, and couldn't hold the gun steady enough to fix Gallup in his sights. He wanted to squeeze the trigger anyway, do something, anything, to vent the fury boiling inside him, but it was useless and he knew it.

He got to his feet, shook his fist, and shouted, "You're a dead man, Gallup. I see you again, you're a dead man. You hear me?"

His voice rolled across the valley, then echoed back at him, its words garbled, half hidden under the pounding of the hooves as Gallup and his two friends raced across the valley floor. He hadn't recognized either man, but it didn't take much imagination to paint their faces in his mind's eye. They had to be Cody Fallon and Jim Anderson. As far as Brady was concerned, there was no one else it could be.

And now he knew it was anything but over.

15

BRADY GOT RID OF the horse carcass before
sunup, using the wagon team to drag it down into
the brush along the creek in the bottom of the next
valley. He couldn't face the prospect of telling
Molly what had happened. Her face was already
drawn with worry, her lips taut as a pair of baling
wires; no matter how she tried to pretend other-
wise, she was still apprehensive. No, this was not
something to add to her trouble. He would find a
way to handle it on his own.

After breakfast, he rode into town, unsure
whether he was going to mention the incident to
Matt Lowry, but by the time he reached the edge
of Nogales, he knew he wasn't going to say a
thing. There was nothing Lowry could do. Maybe
a ride by once in a while, but that would be all but
useless.

In his head, he replayed the hearing, and knew that his identification of Gallup was weak, that there was no other evidence against him, and that Judge Harrison would be no more likely to hold Gallup than he had been Cody Fallon. If Gallup was going to be straightened out, Brady would have to do it.

He bought a couple of boxes of .44 shells for the Colt, and two for the Winchester, the same caliber but with a heavier powder charge. He couldn't practice near the house without telling Molly why, so he rode on out of the south edge of town, into the rolling hills. He knew a box canyon where he could spend a little time looking down the sights of the rifle without attracting any attention from any of the local busybodies. Getting the Colt out of the house was tricky, but he managed. Now he would have to take one step at a time, try to get comfortable with the thought of a pistol in his hand, get his eye back and, eventually, start wearing the gun on his hip.

Brady had thought about picking up a few empty bottles for target practice, but the request was likely to raise a few eyebrows he preferred not be raised. Instead, he brought along some paper and a carpenter's pencil. He'd fashion a couple of paper targets. To attach them to trees, he had a pocket full of barbed-wire staples.

As he rode into the box canyon, he felt as if he

were doing something wrong, that by keeping things secret he was cheating somehow, but there didn't seem to be any other course open to him. The first time Gallup and his friends had paid a nighttime visit, he'd been taken by surprise. Last night, too, had been unexpected. He should have known better, but he hadn't wanted to believe there was anything to fear. But now he was through letting Gallup have the initiative. Now he was going to put things back on level ground.

Dismounting, he tethered his horse to a scrub oak, then found a slab of stone broad enough to accommodate the paper. He sat on the rock, feeling the heat of the morning sun through his jeans. It was quiet in the canyon, a few birds twittering in the trees along a creek and, at the far end, the mutter of a waterfall that spilled rather than fell into the canyon from the rimrock a hundred feet above the canyon floor.

He inscribed three rough circles, darkened them by repeated tracings with the blunt lead point of the carpenter's pencil, put the first target aside and quickly made two more. When he was finished, he tucked the pencil into his shirt pocket and looked for suitable locations to pin the targets. He wanted difficult shots, not because he was proud of his marksmanship, which had been good enough during the war, but because he wanted to push himself, extend his rusty skill quickly to its limit. He wasn't interested in speed, because the war had taught him that accuracy was far more important.

On the leafless hulk of an ancient alder, using a rock and three staples, he tacked the first target about waist high, stooping to make sure that it would be visible over the brush around the base of the tree when he returned to his shooting position. The second he placed another twenty yards farther away, this time standing on tiptoe to reach the top of the target as he nailed it to the trunk of an aspen. The third target he placed thirty yards beyond the second. He guessed the range to be nearly a hundred yards from his position.

He backed away, taking in the quiet beauty of the canyon. The trees, except for the dead alder, were well watered by the creek and their leaves a lush, shiny green. Clumps of grass studded the open, sandy spots among the rocks, and some stretches of grass were thick as carpets and brilliant green in the light spilling over the rimrock. Splashes of color from lupine and paintbrush, columbine and hollyhock drew bees that darted past him as he sauntered back to the spot where he'd left the Winchester.

The canyon smelled of the flowers, especially of the honeysuckle spilling down over the rocks and climbing the walls all around him, and as he reached the flat rock where the rifle lay like a grim reminder of his purpose, he felt guilty that soon the air would stink of gunpowder. It seemed to him like a profanation of such a peaceful setting, but it was why he was there. He picked up the rifle, opened a box of shells, and slipped ten into the magazine, the click of each cartridge sounding louder than it should have in the silence around him.

He dropped to his right knee, looked for the nearest target, found it, and held his aim until his hands stopped shaking. Only when he was comfortable staring down the barrel did he pull the trigger. The recoil of the heavy .44 caliber gun made his shoulder hurt a little, and he rubbed it, listening to the echo of the first shot die away. He was in no hurry, and waited for the swirl of gunsmoke to dissipate before aiming a second time.

He worked the lever to eject the empty shell, sighted in again, and again held his fire. He took a deep breath, trying to will himself into a tranquility circumstances would not permit him. Exhaling slowly, he once more pulled the trigger and this time thought he heard the thwack of the bullet as it struck. He wasn't certain he'd hit the target but thought he'd at least nicked the bark on the dead alder.

Letting the stock of the Winchester down to the sand, he squinted through the bright sun at the nearest of his targets, trying to see whether he'd found the mark. Fighting the urge to go look, he brought the rifle back up, and aimed and squeezed in one fluid movement. The recoil still made his shoulder ache, but this time he'd seen the paper puff out and the round black hole the bullet made as it slammed into the paper near the top of the largest circle.

Working smoothly now, he worked the lever, aimed, and fired. Again, he had the satisfaction of hitting the target, this time inside the middle circle. He was starting to feel it now, and the swirling gunsmoke started to smell good to him, its sharp tang cutting through the flowery fragrance, biting his nostrils, making them tickle. He wiped a trickle of sweat from the tip of his nose, aimed, and fired once more.

He emptied the magazine in continuous fire, then got to his feet, and walked toward the alder. He could see two places where the bark had been chipped, and six holes in the paper. That meant there were two complete misses. The last few rounds had been fairly close together, almost bunched around the edge of the innermost circle. Extracting the pencil, he circled each bullet hole to help keep an accurate account of his progress, then walked back to the rifle.

He kicked the empty shells aside, sat down on the slab of red rock, and reloaded. The magazine held fifteen, but he was going to keep on using ten shells at a time, just to make counting easier. When the last shell clicked home, he looked up at the rimrock and saw a coyote watching him. The animal was poised on a slab of stone perilously close to the edge, its tail wagging.

For a moment, he thought about taking a shot at it, but thought better of it and turned his attention back to the business at hand. On the second load, he concentrated on the middle target, increasing the distance, and trying not to waste his shots. He was feeling more comfortable now, getting used to the heavy Winchester, so different from the musket he had carried in the war. He tried to remember the last time he'd fired a gun with such concentration, and realized it was nearly ten years. He'd hunted, and there had been the occasional urge for target practice, just to keep his hand in, but the Winchester was starting to feel like an extension of his body now, as if his bones had turned to steel and the weapon had been welded to him so securely that he couldn't have put it down even if he wanted to. But the fact was that he didn't want to. He was starting to enjoy it.

The second target posed less difficulty than the first, now that he was used to the weapon, and he was reasonably sure that every shot had found the target—some just barely, but at least he hadn't missed, as near as he could tell. When the rifle was empty, he got up almost eagerly, sprinting into the brush like a little boy, and when he reached the trunk of the aspen, he laughed out loud as he counted the bullet holes, circling each one as he had on the first target and counting them in a loud voice that echoed off the walls of the canyon. Ten hits, some of them marginal, but he'd found the target all ten times. He was almost jubilant now, and couldn't wait to run back and reload for his assault on the third target.

When he was ready, he began firing as rapidly as he could, counting each shot as he pulled the trigger, shouting in exultation when he thought he'd found the mark and, twice, cursing a blue streak when he thought he'd missed. When he had emptied the rifle the third time, he brought it with him into the brush, counted the holes, and found that he had not been as accurate as he had wanted to believe. He had hit the target only six times, six out of ten shots, and two of those were marginal.

Angry and disappointed, he circled the hits so vigorously that he tore the target in two places, and mumbled all the way back to his stash of ammunition. But he wasn't about to pack it in. After reloading, he leaned the gun against the stone. He needed to get his mind off his work for a few minutes and come back with renewed concentration. He walked into the brush, past the most distant target, until he came to the creek, knelt on the sand, and immersed his face in the cold water. He rubbed his cheeks to get the stink of gunsmoke off his skin, then took in a mouthful of the cool water and spat it in an arc that glittered like liquid silver as it splashed back into the creek. A small perch darted toward the bubbles for a moment, then switched its tail and disappeared.

A small blue stone on the bottom caught his eye, and he rolled up his sleeve before plunging his arm in up past the elbow to snatch it from the sand. He rolled it around on his wet palm with the tips of his fingers, thinking Kathleen would love it. Whenever he and Brian went fishing, which wasn't half often enough, Kathleen always reminded them to keep an eye peeled for additions to her collection. She collected pretty stones that she called her "clown jewels" and hoarded them in an old cigar box Brady had gotten from Wes Fraser.

At the thought of the murdered storekeeper, the joy went out of him like air leaking from a balloon. He tucked the blue stone into his pocket and rolled his sleeve back down with quiet deliberation, concentrating on each roll of the cotton as if it were the most important thing he'd ever done.

Buttoning the sleeve, he patted his pocket again to make certain the stone was still there, then got to his feet and started back toward the gun. He stopped at each of the targets to darken the circles with another pass or two of the pencil, telling himself that he would need to draw a few more circles on each of them after the next round of practice.

This time, he fired at each target in turn, rotating through a magazine load of nine shells, then reloading and doing it all over again, then a third time. Only when he had fired three full magazines did he put the gun aside. His ears buzzed with the constant thunder, and a pall of gunsmoke hung in the still air over his head like a gathering storm.

As he walked into the brush, he knew he hadn't missed this time, not once, and when he reached the first target, he saw that he had bunched his shots in a tight cluster that had torn the center out of the stiff paper. They were clustered so tightly that he had difficulty telling one bullet hole from another, but the full complement of ten holes was there, as he had promised himself.

It was the same at each of the remaining two targets. His eye was coming back in a hurry. But the rifle was easy compared to the pistol. Brady walked back to the rock, took three more sheets of paper, and fashioned three more targets. These he positioned at much closer range. The handgun was far more difficult to fire accurately, and it had never been his long suit to begin with.

But circumstances dictated that he try to develop a reasonable level of skill. The reality was that if he was going to be close enough to his targets to use the Colt, he would already be in big trouble, because the numbers were certain to be against him. But Brady was hardheaded enough to think that, no matter what happened, he was not going down without a fight, if it came to that. He hoped it wouldn't, hoped that somehow Gallup would see the pointlessness of continuing to harass a man who posed no threat to him, or that Cody Fallon would somehow remember what happened and have the courage to tell Matt Lowry. Hope was his only ally at the moment, and he'd seen hopes dashed more often than not. If the choice came down to one between hope and a steady hand, he wanted the Colt solid as a rock in his right hand.

An hour later, his hand aching from the kick of the Colt, his shoulder tired from holding the big .44 steady, he figured he was as ready as he was ever going to be.

As he mounted up, he looked around at the canyon, the flowers as colorful as ever, their fragrance a thing of the past. The stench of gunsmoke had taken care of that.

16

BRADY KEPT HIS SECRET, and Molly seemed to be settling down. She still jumped at unexpected noises, and her sleep was restless, but the tautness was gone from her face. It was difficult for Brady to talk about some things, and Molly was as closed as he was in her own way, so for the next two days the subject of Wes Fraser and his killers somehow never seemed to come up.

For those same two days, adopting a more leisurely pace, Brady worked on the barn, putting up the last half of the fourth wall. He spent the better part of one afternoon building doors. Getting them to hang properly was more difficult than he had thought it would be. The enormous strap hinges gleamed dully, their blued steel smelling faintly of oil as he drove home the twelve-penny nails that would hold them in place, and when the last nailhead flattened against the metal of the hinge, he kicked the supports out from under the doors and tugged them open, feeling a sense of accomplishment that seemed exaggerated to him. But he couldn't help but jump in the air and call for Molly to come see.

She came out carrying a bottle of beer for him, a cup of coffee for herself, and a plate of bread and roast beef, a dab of mustard smeared on one edge of the plate. She grinned for the first time in a week, sat on the top step of the porch, and patted the wood beside her. "Come, sit down," she said. "You can admire it from here just as well."

Brady took off his apron, tossed it to one side, and swatted the sawdust from his jeans before walking over to join her. Moving the plate of food, he snatched up the beer bottle, took a long pull on it, and wiped the foam from his lips with his shirtsleeve.

"What do you think?" he asked, waving grandly toward the barn.

She shrugged. "I don't know. What is it?"

For a split second, he thought she was serious, and when it dawned on him that she was teasing, he wrapped her in a bear hug and pushed her over onto the porch floor. She struggled to free herself, cackling so hard she could barely breathe. "You actually were going to answer me, weren't you? You were going to tell me it was a barn. I know you were."

To stop her teasing, he pressed his lips against hers. He mumbled through the kiss, "Think you're smart, don't you?"

She nipped his lip with her teeth, and when he pulled away, she said, "I *know* I am." Sitting up, she asked, "When do you start painting?"

Brady shrugged. "Tomorrow, I guess. I have to get the paint first, and a couple of brushes."

"Why a couple. You don't seriously think I'm going to paint, do you?"

But she was grinning again. Her hair was mussed from the tussle, and she swiped a few stray strands to get them away from her face. "It looks perfect, Dan."

"Really? You think so?"

She nodded. "I do, yes. I mean, I don't know how you did it, and so fast."

Brady shook his head. "I don't either. But thank God it's done. I was starting to think I'd never get it finished."

He slapped some of the roast beef on a slice of bread, spread some mustard on it, then covered it with another thick slice of the warm bread. Taking a bite, he got to his feet, grabbed the beer bottle again, and, holding both in his left hand, reached down with his right until Molly took it. "Come on," he said, pulling her to her feet, "Push those doors around a little bit. See how they move. They're perfect."

Tilting her head with a skeptical smile, she said, "How does one decide that a barn door is perfect?"

"One builds it oneself, one does. And gets an enormous splinter in the palm of one's hand, flattens a thumb and a finger with the hammer and . . ."

"At the same time?"

"I managed." Brady laughed, took another bite of the sandwich, and washed it down with another swallow of warm beer.

Molly followed him to the doors, and he stood back and watched while she swung first one and then the other open, then closed them again. They moved silently, without even a squeak from the well-oiled hinges. "Nice," she said.

"It's better than nice. It's magnificent. That barn'll still be standing when you and I are both long in the grave."

"That's a pleasant thought," she said. "Maybe it'll become a monument. And people will come and lay wreaths on our birthdays."

Brady swallowed the last of his sandwich, finished his beer, and set the bottle on the ground, then walked to the doors and yanked them open, letting them swing wide and bang against the walls of the barn. "Come on inside," he said. He entered the barn, without waiting for an answer. He was standing in the middle of the floor when she joined him. The sharp tang of raw timber filled the cavernous interior.

Here and there, a narrow band of light filtered through joints in the walls where the boards didn't quite meet. In the brilliant sun bands, specks of dust danced like fireflies. Brady pointed out the stalls for livestock, the hayloft, a rack he'd made for tack. "I can't wait until we can get a couple of cows and sheep for the kids. Brian'll love having his own cow to milk. And Kathleen'll spend all her free time out here, I think. As it is, she spends every chance she gets with that snake of hers. We might even have to chain her in bed at night, to keep her away."

"Aren't you making a little more of this than it deserves, Dan? It's a beautiful barn, to be sure, but it seems like you've got more than just sweat invested in it."

"Maybe so. I guess I am. But I finally feel like this place is ours, Moll. It's just the beginning. Maybe we can build a place like Clay Riddle's someday. I mean, we're young enough yet, we're not afraid of hard work, and . . ." he shrugged as if helpless to continue.

"And what?"

"I don't know. I guess I just want everything to be perfect, is all."

"Not just the barn?"

Brady laughed. He walked toward her, encircled

her waist with one arm, and leaned his forehead down to touch hers. "I know you miss Ohio," he said. "But this'll be better, you'll see. You just have to give it some time. You'll love it, if you'll just let yourself. I know you will."

"Dan, I . . ."

"I know what you're going to say, but don't. Just wait. Next spring, when the hills are covered with flowers and the tops of the mountains are still covered with snow, you'll think you've died and gone to heaven. You remember how beautiful it was here last spring?"

She nodded. "I remember."

"Well, just think what it'll be like, year after year. All those lupines and violets, the sound of the bees, and every time the wind blows, the smell of honeysuckle coming in through the windows. It's everything we could ever want, and we're well on our way, now. It'll only get better. The barn's just the beginning. In fact," he said, giving her a lascivious grin, "there's already a little hay in the loft. And . . ."

"Oh, no you don't, Dan Brady!"

"It would sort of christen the place, Moll. Besides, our first time was in a hayloft, if I remember right."

"That was my father's hayloft. And you do remember right. But we're old enough to know better than that, now. It's one thing to risk letting your

parents catch you, quite another when it's your
own children who might . . ."

"It was worth a shot," he said, still grinning.

Unwilling to pour cold water on his enthusiasm,
she squeezed him, tilted her head back, and
reached up to pinch his nose with her fingertips.
"You think so, do you Mr. Brady?"

"You bet I do." He kissed her forehead. "But I
guess I better get into town and get that paint. I
want to start first thing in the morning."

Bright and early the next day, the two of them
were ready, Dan wearing his oldest jeans, Molly a
baggy pair of Dan's pants that she had to roll up
several inches to keep from tripping over the cuffs,
held up by an old belt with an extra hole to keep
them from falling around her ankles. It took them
four days, but when they were almost finished, the
barn gleamed bright red in the afternoon sun.

The whole valley seemed filled with the smell of
paint and solvent, but it was done, and Molly, despite her reservations, had slowly come to share
Dan's enthusiasm. They had saved the doors for
last, and Dan had challenged Molly to a race. She
finished first and backed away to watch her husband cover the last couple of square feet. Both of
them were speckled red from head to toe, and Dan
had one red eyebrow where he'd leaned too close
to the wall to reach up under the eaves.

When he finished his door, he dropped the brush into the paint can, wiped his hands on a rag, and sighed. "That was harder than I thought it would be," he said. "My arm feels like it's about to fall off."

"I'm not sure I like the color," Molly said. "Maybe we should have . . ."

"You can't be serious!" He whirled around, stopping in his tracks when he saw the broad grin.

"Got you again," she said.

Shaking his head, he went into the barn and came back with a large can of spirits and a couple of rags. Opening the can, he soaked one of the rags and started to wipe the paint from his wrists and forearms. Molly took the rag and dabbed at his cheeks and forehead, rubbing his eyebrow roughly to get the clotted paint loose.

He returned the favor, although she seemed to have managed to stay out of harm's way far more skillfully than he. Her hands and arms were spotted, but there was not a drop on her face. "I don't know how you managed to stay so clean," he muttered.

"You're just jealous that I'm a better painter than you are. And faster, too."

"You probably cheated. I don't know how, but I'm sure you did."

She smiled mysteriously. "I'll never tell."

After dinner, they fell into bed like two people

racing one another off a cliff, so tired that their goodnights were little more than mumbles. Brady draped an arm over Molly's shoulders and tried to whisper something in her ear, but his lips went numb, and before he knew it he was out.

When he felt something tugging on his leg, he kicked at it, muttering that it was too early to get up, but the tug grew more insistent, and he realized that it was Brian trying to wake him. He sat up groggily, surprised that it was light already. He glanced toward the window, noticing the strange cast of the light as Brian repeated something for the third time.

"Daddy, Daddy, the barn, the barn!"

"What Brian? What about the barn?"

"Fire!"

Brady felt as if he'd been hit with a hammer. He jumped out of bed, his aching muscles reluctant to cooperate, and limped to the window. He could see now that the barn was ablaze, one wall a sheet of orange flame. Black smoke mushroomed over the roof, and flames, their appetites whetted by the fresh paint, were already beginning to slaver across the shingles in ravenous tongues. He ran back to the bed, shook Molly awake, and yanked on his boots.

Yelling over his shoulder for her to hurry, Brady ran outside, raced to the well, and started to work the pump like a man possessed. When he had a bucketful of water, he ran to the barn and hurled it as high as he could. On the hill behind the barn, he saw the outline of a man on horseback and thought he would soon have some help. He raced back as the water hissed and boiled against the blazing wall. Again he worked the pump, and saw Molly running toward him.

Her face was a pale mask, her eyes huge and dark in the orange light. "What happened? My God, what . . . ?"

"Grab the pail, Moll." When he handed her the bucket, he saw its weight make her body sag as he let go. He raced to the house for another bucket, and she was back by the time he returned to the pump. He jerked the pump handle as fast as he could, filling one pail, shoving it aside for her, and kicking the second under the spout.

Over and over, they repeated the process, Brady, because he was stronger, working the pump, Molly staggering back and forth under the weight of the heavy pails, in her haste sloshing almost as much water onto the ground as she managed to hurl at the flames.

"I can't get the water high enough," she wailed on her next trip. "It's too high up."

Brian was trying to help, but there wasn't much he could do. Suddenly, Molly screamed, "Kathleen? Where are you? Kathleen?"

She looked at Brady, who froze at the pump,

every nerve in his body suddenly screaming. "Brian, where's your sister?"

The boy shook his head.

"The snake," Brady shouted. "She's gone for the snake . . ."

Molly ran to the open door of the barn and disappeared inside, Brady right behind her. A wall of heat slammed him like a heavy fist. Smoke swirled in serpentine strands, thick, wriggling ropes of black against the air full of gray. Molly called out from somewhere in the roiling smoke, "Kathleen?"

"Here, Mommy. Here!"

"Where, honey? Where are you?"

Brady grabbed Molly around the waist. "Get outside, Moll. I'll get her."

Something cracked high overhead, and part of the roof caved in, filling the smoky hell with red light. Molly broke free from his embrace and ran in circles like a madwoman. Brady, knowing where the crate with Kathleen's snake was kept, ran for it and found Kathleen, the wooden crate cradled in her arms.

He picked up his daughter and started for the door.

Another explosion filled the barn with a shower of sparks. A great groan, as if the earth were cracking in two, filled the barn, and Brady thought he could feel the ground heaving under his feet. He raced for the door, groping blindly with one hand, Kathleen dangling against his hip.

He stumbled and fell, lost his grip for a moment, then grabbed Kathleen by the arm, and tugged her forward, crawling. He felt his fingernails cracking, filling with dirt from the hard-packed floor. Heat seared through his underwear, and he felt as if it were ready to burst into flame. Sparks like warring comets darted in every direction. Then came another crack, this one louder than the last, like a bomb going off.

The rafters were starting to give way now. He could just make out the outline of the doorway, and he pulled and shoved and clawed his way into the open away from the scorching heat, the choking clouds of smoke. Kathleen still had her crate, and she sat down, put it in her lap, and started to cry softly.

Brady started for the pump, knowing even as he took his first step that it was too late. He stopped then, puzzled. "Moll?"

Where was she? He ran to Brian, who was trying to work the pump. "Where's your mom?"

Brian shook his head, and Brady turned toward the inferno. He started to run, reaching the door as another rafter gave way. He wrapped a forearm around his face and started to grope into the smoke. "Moll? Moll?"

Thunder rolled out of the open doorway, a great

puff of smoke swirling around him, and he knew from the noise that the loft had given way.

"Moll?" A whisper. Then a scream, "Molly? Molly? Molly?"

There was no answer.

17

BRADY DROVE THE RUDE cross into the ground just above the end of the mound of dark earth already beginning to lighten as the sun beat down on it. With every blow of the hammer, his rage pulsed inside him like a beat struggling to break through flesh and bone that was too frail to contain it.

When he was done, he tossed the hammer high into the air, watched it arc overhead, flashing in the sun as it turned over lazily once, then again, an finally saw it plummet earthward like a thunderbolt from Thor. It landed in the ruins of the barn, but instead of shattering the ground, it hit with a dull thud, kicked up a puff of ashes, and scattered a few embers, a feeble end to his dreams.

He knelt down, pulled the children close, draping an arm around each, squeezed them so hard he was afraid he might crush them, then got to his feet. Kathleen had a flower in her hand, one plucked from Molly's garden beside the house, and when Dan leaned over to kiss his daughter on the top of her head, she bent down, stabbed the columbine's fragile stem into the soft mound, and fell on her knees. Brian knelt beside her, put an arm around his sister, and tried to comfort her.

Brady was not good at prayer, a pastime for which he had little but contempt. He'd heard too many that had gone unanswered to bother. But for Molly's sake, on the off chance it mattered, he mumbled, "Lord, keep her safe. Protect her better than I did." He looked up at the sky, then back at the mound of earth and, as an afterthought, added, "Thank you."

He didn't want to tear the children away from the grave, but he had things to do, things that wouldn't wait, that couldn't wait. He bent forward, grabbed each of them around the waist, and lifted them up. Brian struggled, kicking and crying, but Kathleen squirmed around to face him, and buried her face in his chest. Her tiny body shook with silent sorrow as he carried them to the house.

In twenty minutes, he was ready. Brian noticed the gunbelt, looked up at his father, his eyes wet and red rimmed, the question he couldn't ask in his eyes. Then, as if he were frightened of the answer, he closed his trembling lids and grabbed Brady around the waist.

Brady went outside, hitched the team to the wagon, its tail end scorched black from having been parked too close to the barn during the blaze. He'd done his packing early, even before digging Molly's grave, because he had known even then what he was going to do. Now all that remained was to do it. He lifted the children into the wagon seat, tied his chestnut to the tailgate, and climbed up into the wagon.

He released the brakes, snapped the reins, and headed down the lane toward the road. He looked back once, averting his eyes from the house and concentrating his attention on the heap of blackened timbers. Small, pale gray tendrils of viney smoke climbed over the charred ruins and were lost at once in the sunlight.

It took an hour to reach Ray Berry's place, and when the wagon creaked into the front yard, Rachel came out onto the porch, her surprised face squinting into the bright morning sun. "Dan?" she asked. "Whatever are you doing here?"

He climbed down from the wagon, helped Brian and then Kathleen to the ground, and sent them off to play with Ray and Rachel's two daughters. Only then was he ready to try to put into words what had happened, what he needed from his friends. "Molly's . . ." But he wasn't ready. He choked on the words, and tears started to trickle down his cheeks.

Rachel rushed toward him, calling for her husband. "Raymond? Raymond, come quick!"

Brady chewed his lower lip, broke the skin, and felt the blood ooze down his chin.

"Dan, what is it? What's happened?"

Brady inhaled, felt his whole body tremble, and squeezed the breath from his lungs, hoping it would take the sorrow and the pain along with it. "Molly's gone," he said.

Ray Berry came running from the open door of his barn. Rachel turned, looking alternately at both men. Ray, sensing that something was wrong, stopped in his tracks for a second, then walked quickly forward. "Dan," he said. "Something wrong?"

Rachel, not sure what Brady had meant, looked at him expectantly. And Brady had another chance to try to put it into words. "Molly's dead," he said, his body shaking.

Rachel, as if the reality had finally dawned on her, raised a hand to her mouth. "Oh, my God . . ."

"Jesus Christ, Dan, what happened?"

Brady told them about the fire, using as few words as possible, waving off question after question. When he'd said about as much as he could stand, he looked at his friends in silence for a moment. "I was wondering . . . could you keep Brian and Kathleen for a few days?"

Rachel threw her arms around him. "Oh, Dan, I'm so sorry . . ."

"What are you going to do?" Ray asked. He rubbed the stubble of whiskers on his chin, then tossed his head to get the long blond hair out of his eyes. "You tell Matt Lowry?"

Brady shook his head. "This is none of Matt's affair."

"You can't handle this by yourself, Dan. You know that."

"I'll handle it, all right."

"You want me to come along?"

Again, Brady shook his head. "No, Ray. Thanks, but this is something I have to do for myself. *By* myself."

Rachel backed away from him then, just a step or two, but Brady knew it meant she disapproved. "You have the children to think about, Dan. You have to let . . ."

"Rachel, leave the man be," Berry cut in. "He let the law handle it, and you see what it got him. He knows what he's doing."

"Thanks, both of you," Brady said. He walked over to where the kids were playing, called Brian and Kathleen to him, and knelt on one knee. "Daddy has to go away for a few days. I want you to be good while you're here. You listen to Mr. and Mrs. Berry, all right?"

Brian nodded dumbly, but Kathleen, sensing something that had escaped her brother, threw her arms around Dan's neck. "You'll come back, won't you, Daddy?"

Brady, too full to speak, nodded. He stroked her

back, felt the bones of her spine, the shaking of her body, the silken strands of her hair, so like her mother's.

Getting to his feet again, he sent the children off with a push, walked back to the wagon, and started to unhitch the team.

"I'll take care of that, Danny," Berry said. "You go on."

Brady backed away from the wagon, walked to the rear, and untied his horse. He swung up into the saddle, shifting his weight slightly to get comfortable. Berry sent Rachel inside, then moved close enough to speak without the children overhearing him. "I expect you'll be starting at Clay Riddle's place?"

Brady nodded.

"Ain't likely Gallup and them stayed around but . . ."

"It doesn't matter. I'll find them. I don't care where they are."

"Them boys stick together, Dan. You be careful. Clay's a good man, and I reckon he'd give you a hand, if you was to ask, but I don't suppose you will."

"No, I won't ask," Brady told him.

"You're sure it was Gallup, ain't you?"

"No doubt in my mind. None whatever. I saw him last night, on the hill behind the barn. I didn't realize it at first, but . . . I know."

Berry nodded. "All right, my friend. I'm not a praying man, but I just might try to put in a word with the good Lord tonight."

Brady smiled distantly. "I don't imagine he'd be disposed to help me, but it can't hurt, I guess. I'll be back as soon as I can. There's a few things for the kids in the back of the wagon, in the valise. And some papers. An address, Molly's sister. She'll take the kids, in case I don't . . ."

"Don't you even think that way, Danny," Berry said, interrupting him. "We'll see you in a few days."

On the ride to Clay Riddle's place, Brady wrestled with his rage. He knew that he had to have a grip on his feelings, had to think clearly, if he was going to get through the next few days. There was a chance, of course, that Gallup would be right there, at the Rolling R, and things would come to a quick end, but somehow he knew it wasn't going to be that simple. That Gallup was responsible for the fire, and probably with help from Anderson and Fallon, was not open to question. But whether the cowboys knew that Molly had been . . . he couldn't take it any further. Not now. Not yet.

The rage inside him was like a lump of white hot metal, heavy in his gut, filling his bones with its heat, sending tongues of fire licking along every nerve, making every muscle twitch. It was consuming him, and he had to find a way to get control of himself. He tried making his mind a blank, wiping out everything except the road ahead of him. But he wasn't that strong.

By the time he crossed the bridge at the foot of the hill beneath Clay Riddle's home, he had come as close as he could to making his mind blank—empty of everything but his purpose, which lurked just beyond the reach of his brain when he tried to focus on it. He rode across the bridge and circled the base of the hill, into the cottonwoods and up toward the bunkhouse.

A handful of horses jostled one another in the corral beyond the bunkhouse, but there appeared to be no one about. He dismounted, snatched his Winchester from the boot, took off the safety, and levered a round into the chamber as he walked toward the front door of the bunkhouse.

He didn't bother to knock, kicking the door open and bursting into the dimness like a gust of cold wind. One man lay on his bunk and sat up rubbing his eyes. Brady pointed the Winchester at him. "You know why I'm here," he said.

The cowboy, a skinny kid with a little peach fuzz on his chin, his sallow skin dotted with red welts, shook his head and ran a hand through lank brown hair. "Hold on, Mister," he said. "How can I know why you're here? I don't even know who the hell you are."

The kid's voice quavered and cracked once as he shrank back against the wall beside his bunk.

"Where's Don Gallup?"

The kid shook his head. "I don't know. Ain't seen him since early this morning. You'll have to ask Mr. Riddle."

"Cody Fallon?"

Again, a head shake.

"Anderson?"

"I'm tellin' you, Mister, I don't know. I ain't been feelin' too good. Got chicken pox. Mr. Riddle's probably to the house. You'll have to ask him."

"I find out you lied to me, I'll be back, boy. You can count on it."

"I ain't lying, Mister. I swear to God."

Brady backed out of the bunkhouse and saw two men approaching on horseback. One of them was Tim Foley. Brady recognized him from his card playing on the bench the last time he'd been there. The other didn't look familiar. Without making any attempt to hide the Winchester, or to put it up, Brady ran toward them. "Foley," he called, "where's Don Gallup?"

Foley reined in a few yards short of him, pushed his hat back, and shifted a straw he had clamped between his teeth. "Last I seen him, he was over toward Fox Mountain. Mr. Riddle sent him and a few other boys over to run down some strays. That was early, but he's probably still there. Donny don't like nothing to take less than a day, if he can help it."

Foley grinned, but Brady didn't return the smile. "You sure about that?"

"Not positive, but if I was lookin' for him, and it sure as hell seems like you are, that's where I'd start."

"Who's with him?"

"Cody Fallon, Pete Domergue, couple other boys. I ain't quite certain who all. I think Clay is over that way, too. You'll probably run into him on the way over. Maybe he can tell you for sure."

"You see Gallup, you tell him Dan Brady is looking for him. And if he owes you any money, you damn well better collect it before I find him."

Brady saw the question on Foley's face, but didn't wait for him to ask it. He sprinted to his horse and vaulted into the saddle, digging his spurs in deep enough to make the big stallion spurt forward. Foley yelled something to him, but Brady ignored him. His mind was elsewhere.

18

THE RIDE TO FOX MOUNTAIN took nearly two hours. Brady was pushing his horse hard, maybe too hard, but he was barely conscious of the strain on the animal. He had his mind fixed on only one thing, and everything else was little more than a blur at the outer edge of his consciousness.

He was still four miles away when he spotted a plume of smoke. More than likely, a branding fire, he thought. Foley had told him that Clay Riddle was out there somewhere, too. He found himself wondering how he was going to handle it if he bumped into the rancher before he found Gallup and Fallon and whoever else. It was the whoever else that brought him up short. He wanted vengeance, that much was indisputable, but how far, he wondered, was he willing to go to exact it? What would happen if Clay Riddle were to get in the way? What would he do if Gallup and Fallon and Anderson were accompanied by other men, men he didn't know, men who may not have known anything about the murder of Wes Fraser . . . or Molly's death?

In his current state, he knew he was not likely to be reasonable. Picking and choosing was not something a madman bothers to do, and Brady was verging on madness. His grief burned in his gut like a ball of molten lead. He could feel it searing him, reducing him, as if it were physically consuming him. And he didn't give a damn. As long as he lasted long enough to put a bullet through Don Gallup's heart, burst that throbbing muscle the same way his own had burst, then nothing else would matter, nothing at all.

And again he had to stop and question himself. What about Brian? What about Kathleen? At the thought of his children, he felt sadness break over him, a smothering wave that threatened to choke him. His throat constricted, and his chest felt as if it were constrained by iron bands. They were hostages now, to Molly's death, to Brady's rage, and to whatever happened to him out there in the middle of nowhere.

For a moment, he wavered, a man teetering on the edge of a cliff. He felt as if he had decided to jump and only then begun to worry what would happen to him when he hit bottom. But gravity would have its way; all he could do was close his eyes and wait to land.

He reached back into his saddlebags and found the binoculars he had filched during the war. Opening the battered leather case, he looped the strap around his neck, tucked the case back into the saddlebags, and trained the glasses on the smoke, following the column down to the ground. He couldn't see the fire, because there was a low hill in the way, but he saw no one around, and figured Gallup and his crew were working on the other side.

Letting the glasses drop against his breastbone, he nudged the chestnut into a trot, keeping his eyes on the smoke and angling to the right. He wanted to get a look into the valley from some distance. The last thing he wanted to do was to ride head on into a work party without knowing the odds.

It took him nearly an hour to work his way down to a creek, which he followed far enough to circle the hill at a point some two miles east of the fire. Dismounting, he hobbled the chestnut, took the Winchester, and started up the slope. Just before he reached the hilltop, he dropped to his stomach, swung the binoculars around to rest them on his back, and crawled the last fifty feet. Lying flat, he eased forward another few feet until he could see into the valley.

The fire was still burning, a stack of wood lying

a few feet away. One man squatted at the fireside, his back to Brady, poking at the fire to stir it up. As Brady watched, the man straightened up, walked to the stack of wood, and grabbed a couple of small logs, walked back, and dropped them unceremoniously into the flames. Even in the brilliant sunlight, Brady saw a cloud of sparks, and the column of smoke mushroomed out for a moment before returning to the wavering strand he had first seen.

Brady watched the man for several minutes, hoping to get a good look at his face, but the cowboy was too busy tending to his chores to look around. On the far side of the fire a small herd of cattle, mostly calves, grazed on the thick grass. Brady examined the calves, looking for some evidence they had been branded, but as near as he could tell, they were unmarked. Their ears hadn't been notched, and their hides had not been seared by the branding iron. Apparently, the work crew was going to round up as many calves and strays as it could and brand them all at once.

Brady smiled grimly as he realized that the men would be coming back, probably one or two at a time. If luck was with him, he might be able to slip in closer and take them on one by one instead of having to confront the whole group at once. But that was putting the cart ahead of the horse. First he had to make sure Gallup, Fallon, and Anderson were there at all.

Too antsy to sit still and wait, Brady backed down the hill and mounted the chestnut. It wouldn't be a bad idea, he thought, to survey the terrain and get some idea of which way to run, if he had to, and where cover was available. He took a circuitous route, edging closer to Fox Mountain, which loomed up out of the rolling hills, four miles away.

The approaches to the mountain were full of blind alleys, canyons, dry washes, and arroyos that wound sometimes a mile or more before running into a blank wall. Some interlaced in a maze carved out of the earth by time and running water. Brady had been in the area four or five times. In the last year, he had run down a couple of dozen wild mustangs to add to his herd, but the network of canyons and gullies would take months to explore, and he'd had neither the interest nor the time. Now, though, he regretted not having paid more attention.

He was more than a mile past the valley where the branding fire and the collected strays were, and as he climbed a rocky hill, he decided to dismount and train the glasses on the fire to see if he could get a better look at the cowboy tending the small herd. Adjusting the focus knob, he watched the man, now leaning back against a boulder, his hat tilted forward over his face to shield his eyes from the sun.

Even without seeing the man's face, he decided it was neither Gallup nor Fallon. Cody Fallon was tall and lean, probably seven or eight inches taller than the sentinel. Gallup was shorter than Fallon, but blocky, muscular, and broad through the chest. Of the three men he sought, only Jim Anderson came close, but Brady couldn't be sure. Anderson was so ordinary in appearance, he'd made almost no impression at all on Brady. He'd know Anderson only if he saw him close up, not from this distance.

The man was still alone, and Brady turned his attention to the interlacing canyons stretching out toward the mountain. Most of the arroyos and washes were shallow, but some of the cuts were seventy or eighty feet deep, a few even deeper, and a man riding along the floor of any of the deeper canyons couldn't be seen except by someone right at the rim. Even so, Brady swept the glasses in a broad arc, looking for any trace that might narrow his search—a cloud of dust, a startled bird, anything at all that might indicate the presence of someone below.

But the terrain was as silent and empty as Brady's heart. Disappointed, he climbed back into the saddle, heading in the general direction of Fox Mountain, off to the northwest. The iron hooves of the chestnut clicked on the rocky ground. Other than the occasional squeak of leather and the jin-

gle of his spurs, it was the only sound. If he were
to rely on his ears, he'd be tempted to think he and
the chestnut were the only living things for ten
miles in any direction.

It was another half hour before he spotted the
dust cloud, shimmering in the sunlight just above
the rim of a canyon a quarter-mile ahead. He dug
in his spurs and pushed the chestnut forward in a
spurt, then walked it a hundred and fifty yards
until he was no more than fifty yards from the rim.
He could hear cattle bellowing, several dozen head
from the sound of it, and the occasional click of
shod hooves on stone.

Dismounting, he unbooted the Winchester and
walked toward the rim, resisting the urge to
crouch, as if it would somehow make real the access of nerves he was trying to tell himself didn't
exist. Ten yards from the rim, he stopped to listen.
He was fifty or sixty yards ahead of the billowing
cloud which welled up and then dipped back
below the rim, like a wave rushing into shallow
water.

Brady heard voices now, two for sure, possibly
more. He walked along the canyon rim, keeping
far enough back so that no one below could see
him, until he was even with the dust cloud. Duck-
ing, he moved closer, hoping to hear one of the
men mention a name, but the conversation was all
directed at the cattle. Over the constant bellowing

of the cows, it was impossible to recognize any of the voices.

Brady dropped to his stomach, crawled the last few feet, and **peered** down into the canyon. The dust was thick in the air, but he could see well enough to recognize Cody Fallon riding drag. Two men, one of whom was almost certainly Jim Anderson, rode on the left wing of the herd. The canyon was only a hundred yards or so wide at this point, and the steers were against the wall directly below him. A fourth man rode point. It was Don Gallup.

Brady took a deep breath. It was tempting to bring the Winchester to bear and open fire. But Brady couldn't force himself to do it. He wanted vengeance, but he wasn't an assassin. He told himself it was because he wanted to look Gallup in the eye and tell him what he thought of him, tell him why he deserved to die. He wanted Gallup to know it was Dan Brady's bullet that tore through his body, broke his bones, and blew a three-inch crater in his cowardly flesh. It would be harder that way, riskier, too, but that was just the way it had to be.

Brady got to his feet, not caring whether anyone saw him, and sprinted back to his horse. He climbed into the saddle, keeping the Winchester out, braced across his thighs as he nudged the horse toward the canyon rim. He fell in behind the cowboys below, feeling suddenly easy, light, as if a great weight had been lifted from him. Able to breathe freely again, he took a great gulp of air and let it out in a sigh of satisfaction. He could feel some of the tension drain away. Now that he'd found Gallup, he realized he had been afraid, not of facing the man but of not finding him. He wanted resolution, he wanted justice, and he wanted revenge. But what he wanted more than he had ever wanted anything in the world was for Don Gallup to pay for what he'd done to Molly.

And now he was going to get the chance to make it happen. He felt his face moving of its own accord, struggled against it, and lost. The grim smile became a mask, one that he knew he would wear until Gallup was dead and not a moment longer.

The terrain ahead was sloping downward. He stayed near the rim, not caring if the men below saw him, half hoping they would. A mile in front of him, the ground flattened out, the canyon to his left emptying into a broad valley. He let the chestnut take its head, in no hurry, knowing that time was never less in his control, content to let the future unfold at its leisure. He had, after all, he reminded himself, nothing else to do.

He was only forty feet above the cowhands now and not more than a couple of hundred yards behind them. The dust continued to swirl up from the milling cattle, a pale beige cloud that seemed to be lit from inside, a glow mysterious as that of a firefly, and just as ephemeral.

With less than a quarter-mile to go before the ground flattened out and Brady would reach the valley floor, Cody Fallon urged his horse ahead, shouting something that Brady could not quite hear, and when he passed the two men on the left wing, they turned. The one he did not know, a chunky man whose three-day growth was caked with trail dust, glanced upward, saw Brady, and said something to Anderson and Fallon. Both hands turned then, followed the directing finger of the unknown man, and, when they spotted Brady, waved, as if he were an old friend. Brady realized they did not recognize him, and he waved back, buying a little time, time to get closer, and he felt the smile broaden a little on his face.

Fallon moved on, reached Gallup, and fell in beside him. Brady continued on, angling a little to the left now, and starting down the last quarter-mile of slope where the canyon wall plunged more sharply, rose again for a hundred yards, then fell all the way to the valley floor. Boulders made the going serpentine, and the horse had to pick its way carefully through the stones. Brady was using the reins now to negotiate the maze of larger rocks.

At the bottom of the slight depression, he lost sight of the small herd for a few minutes, and when he reached the last crest, he saw that they had

gained on him a little. He urged the chestnut on
with his knees, leaning back in the saddle a bit to
compensate for the steepness of his final descent.

When he reached the valley floor, he was a good
five hundred yards behind the herd. Fallon had still
not come back to the drag position, and the wingmen had dropped back a bit to keep the stragglers
moving. Brady still had the Winchester braced
across the saddle horn, checked to make sure that
the safety was off, and narrowed the gap.

Eating dust made his throat dry, and he felt the
dirty film on his lips caking to mud. As he wiped
his mouth with his sleeve, he thought for a moment how Molly would have scolded him for getting so dirty. A wave of sadness rushed up out of
the canyon behind him, swirled around him, and
he felt the paste on his cheeks moisten. His eyes
blurred and he knew it had nothing to do with the
dust in the air. Blinking away the moisture, he once
again wiped his face with his sleeve and glanced at
the dark brown smears on the faded cotton. His
tongue traced the contours of his mouth, and he
leaned over and spat out the muddy dust.

He was only three hundred yards behind now,
and closing. At two hundred yards, the wingmen
glanced back. Brady could see them talking to one
another, and they fell off the tail end of the herd
and wheeled their mounts. They were heading
straight toward him now, Jim Anderson and the

man he did not know. There were nearly fifty
steers, and the dust was so thick he could not see
Fallon or Gallup at the front.

Anderson recognized him when they were less
than fifty yards away. He shouted something, and
the man Brady had never seen spurred his horse
forward as Anderson reined in. The cowboy
leaned forward, and Brady saw the stock of a rifle
in his hand, then saw the barrel clear the boot. Anderson, too, went for his gun, grabbing a Colt
from his holster. Brady swung his Winchester
around as the cowboy tried to aim his own rifle.

Brady jerked the reins hard, leaped from the saddle, and dropped to one knee as the cowboy fired.
The bullet whistled close to Brady's ear as he
sighted down the barrel of his rifle, sucked in a
deep breath, and squeezed.

This was not like shooting at paper tacked to a
tree. This was a target of flesh and bone, and as he
heard the wet smack of his .44 caliber slug against
the cowboy's chest, his nerves began to hum. He
hadn't felt like that since The Wilderness, and his
hands trembled as he watched the cowboy lean far
back in the saddle, then tumble as his horse bolted,
charging straight toward Brady. The cowboy dangled from one stirrup, then his foot pulled free, and
the horse thundered past, close enough for Brady
to reach out and touch his dusty flank.

As Brady looked for Anderson, he heard the

whistle of a bullet high over his head and then the crack of Anderson's Colt, a dull, flat sound in the open space. Brady struggled to hold the Winchester steady as he homed in on Anderson, but Anderson's horse reared up and turned sharply like a bucking bronc, and before Brady could find his second target, the big roan spurted forward and was lost in the swirling dust for a second, reappearing as a murky shadow. Brady aimed quickly and fired, knowing as he pulled the trigger that his aim was wide. Then Anderson was gone.

Brady ran for his horse, and as he climbed into the saddle a flurry of pistol shots exploded in the dirty haze. It took him a few seconds to realize that Anderson was trying to drive the cattle back toward him, and a few seconds more before the first of the frightened animals materialized out of the whirling dust, bleating in terror. It was followed by several more, and Brady was forced to turn the chestnut and run for the opposite wall, out of the path of the charging cattle.

Clear of the dust against the far wall, he saw three horsemen lashing their mounts and running for the mountains. Gritting his teeth, he shouted one agonizing, unintelligible shriek, then kicked the chestnut hard and galloped after them.

19

BY THE TIME Brady was in full gallop, the three cowboys had a substantial lead on him. He drove the chestnut hard, but the three cow ponies had stamina and were more used to running hard in open country. It was all Brady could do to keep the three men in sight.

It was already late afternoon, and he knew that if he didn't catch them before sundown, he might lose them altogether. Another possibility was that they might have time to gather reinforcements, and Brady was determined not to let that happen. He wanted Gallup for himself. He'd seen too much of the law, seen how easily Gallup had walked away from Wes Fraser's murder, and he'd die before he let it happen again. *This time, Mr. Gallup,* he thought, *you will pay the piper.*

He had the sense that he was hanging close, perhaps even gaining a bit on the men, but the ground was getting rocky, and the slight upward tilt of the terrain was making it even harder for the big chestnut. Staying even uphill was one thing, making up the huge lead was another.

At times, he lost sight of the three fugitives altogether and was forced to mark their flight by the dust kicked up by their mounts. That they had chosen to run rather than fight was worrisome. He thought they might be leading him into an ambush, but all he could do to guard against the possibility was keep his eyes open and his wits about him. He realized, too, that they might think he had men with him, either the sheriff or a few friends willing to throw a rope around their necks and run them up the nearest tree like so many flags of raw meat.

But Brady was certain of one thing—innocent men didn't run, not when the odds were in their favor. The flight merely confirmed their guilt in Brady's mind, and made him more determined than ever to deliver his own brand of justice. They would pay, not just for Molly, but for Wes Fraser, too, for all the pain Sarah Fraser was suffering, for Brady's own pain, and for the bleak, motherless future of Brian and Kathleen. They were kids, innocent kids, and they didn't deserve to suffer. But Gallup had inflicted on them a pain that would never end and that might never even dwindle away to a dull ache in the heart. The thought of Kathleen whimpering in the night, wrestling with the enormity of her loss like Jacob with an angel, flashed through his brain like a meteor, and he cursed Gallup over and over again, the words settling into the pounding rhythm of the chestnut's hooves.

The sky caught fire as thin clouds swept in front to the northwest, caught the sunlight, and fractured it into a dozen shades of red and orange. In an hour or so, it would start to get dark, and Brady felt the pressure of the receding daylight. His horse was tired, and he was exhausted too, having slept little the night before. But he couldn't let himself give in to the temptation to wait.

The foothills at the base of Fox Mountain and the slopes of the mountain itself were heavily wooded, but the intervening country was rocky and barren. The grass was already beginning to thin, and the dry earth beneath it was baked hard by the sun and covered with a thin layer of powdery dust. Brady could still track the fugitives by the clouds kicked up by their mounts, but if he lost sight of them, finding them again would be a nightmare. Brady was no tracker, and in the terrain that lay ahead, it would take a man with the eye of an Apache to follow them.

In spite of the ache in his back and shoulders, the exhaustion that threatened to sweep over him like a flood, he pushed on still harder. He still

didn't know what Gallup and the other two men
were planning, whether they would be content to
run until they lost him, or if they were heading
someplace definite, where they could turn and
make a stand. He hoped it was the latter, because
he had no intention of giving up, and the sooner he
got it over with, the sooner he could get back to
the children.

There was still more than a mile to the leading
edge of the forest, where the dust would no longer
help him, and where the thick carpet of fallen needles from the dense pines would yield not a trace
of a hoofprint. By the time the sun started to go
down, it was apparent the cowboys were going to
bypass the mountain, perhaps afraid that they
would be trapped on its higher reaches with
nowhere to turn. They veered west, keeping to the
open country and riding along the edge of the forest to make better time than they could among the
trees. It seemed an odd choice, and made Brady
nervous, but there was no point in second-guessing
himself now.

He used the binoculars while there was still
enough light and watched the three riders move
into the broad mouth of a wide canyon, its walls
towering over them on either side, the sheer cliffs
rising more than two hundred feet into the air in
some places. Brady was fifteen or twenty minutes
behind them now, and when he lost sight of them

as the canyon closed around them, he spurred the chestnut hard one more time.

It was getting dark rapidly now, the clouds thickening and choking off the dying sunlight until Brady could no longer see more than a few hundred feet ahead. In less than a half hour, he'd be down to a walk.

By the time he reached the mouth of the canyon it was dark. He dismounted, curled the reins in his hand, and tugged the tired chestnut forward until he was just inside the canyon's maw. He stopped then and held the stallion steady, patting its nose and holding the reins short to keep it still.

No sound came from the yawning darkness. Brady knew there was a chance the cowboys had kept on moving, but he couldn't risk riding into an ambush. He walked toward the right-hand wall of the canyon, found a scrub oak, and tethered the stallion securely, then took the Winchester from its boot and moved deeper into the canyon. He stayed close to the wall, moving as quickly as he dared in the darkness. The base of the wall was piled with broken rock, huge slabs that had fallen from the towering walls, and mounds of loose stone that rattled when kicked and creaked under the soles of his boots.

He had never been there before, had no idea how long the canyon might be or where it led. It was a hell of a time to find out, but he had no choice. Once, he tripped over a stone slab, scraped his shin on its edge, and felt blood trickle down into his boot where the skin had been scraped away by the sharp edge of the rock.

Ignoring the pain, he cursed under his breath and he got to his feet, moved a bit away from the wall to make his passage a little easier, and picked up his pace a bit. In the dark, it was hard to judge how far he'd gone, but he estimated nearly half a mile. The canyon was narrow in places, snaked between its walls, twists and turns coming so fast sometimes that he felt as if he were walking in a circle.

He stopped every hundred feet or so, thinking perhaps to overhear a scrap of careless conversation. But all he could hear was his own breathing, its rasp like a high wind in the silence. It was another five hundred yards before he saw the light, an orange flicker dancing on the walls. He stopped then, listened, and heard the mutter of a restless horse. His heart began to pound as he moved forward, certain he had found his quarry.

The light continued to rise and fall, and twice he saw a shadow that appeared to be the shape of a man momentarily glide across the broken stone towering above him. For a moment, he wanted to charge ahead, force a conclusion to the terrible anxiety that tore at his flesh like a thousand thorns, but he controlled himself, forced himself to breathe deeply to calm his nerves, then started forward slowly, one foot in front of the other, each placed as quietly as he could manage in the darkness.

The fire was off to his left and seemed to be contained in some sort of enclosure, either a large niche in the wall or perhaps an arm of the canyon. He stayed flush against the right-hand wall until he could see the flames themselves. Once more, he heard a horse, this time a nicker, as if it was nervous about something, perhaps sensing his presence. He heard a voice then, low, mumbling to the animal to be quiet.

Fifty yards later he could see the flames themselves and, beyond them, three horses hobbled against a stone wall. To the left, on the far side of the blaze, were the huddled shapes of three men wrapped in blankets, their backs against the same wall. One of them had a rifle across his knees, but his face was shrouded in shadow, and it wasn't possible to identify him. The other two appeared to be sleeping. He crept closer, thinking he might surprise the sentry and get the drop on all three before they had a chance to react.

He was about to charge in when a catamount snarled somewhere in the darkness, its growl rising to a whine, echoing off the walls and terrifying the horses. All three animals started to buck, trying to free their legs from the hobbles, and one reared up, its whinny every bit as terrifying as the snarl of the big cat. The two sleeping men woke up and tossed off their blankets as the sentry got to his feet. As he moved toward the frightened horses, his face came into sharp relief—Cody Fallon.

Another man moved to the fire carrying a canteen and coffee pot. "No sense trying to sleep tonight," he said. "Might as well make some coffee." He squatted on the far side of the fire, and Brady could see his face clearly. It was Don Gallup.

Brady watched him make coffee, knowing that all chance of surprising the men had gone. He thought about staying where he was, waiting until morning, and hoping that the men would fall asleep sometime before dawn. But it was too risky. He was a mile from his horse, and that was something that could get him killed. For all he knew, Gallup planned on meeting someone there, and the numbers were already in the cowboy's favor. Reluctantly, Brady backed away, keeping his eyes pinned to the opening in the wall until he rounded a bend in the canyon and could no longer see even the flickering glow from the fire.

He walked back to the horse, turning options over in his mind like a man examining a lump of shiny metal, trying to decide whether it was gold or pyrite. And by the time he reached the chestnut, he knew what he was going to do. It was a gamble, but he didn't have a single choice that wasn't one.

Untethering the horse, he climbed into the saddle and wheeled the chestnut around.

At a fast walk, he left the canyon moving nearly a quarter-mile away until he found what he was looking for, a negotiable slope that would allow him to move up top and follow the rimrock. He was betting that Gallup planned to move all the way through the canyon, probably at first light and maybe even before dawn broke. It meant moving cautiously, but when he considered the choices open to him, it seemed the most sensible.

Once he reached the top of the canyon wall, he dismounted, took the reins in his hand, and started to lead the chestnut with gentle tugs. In the darkness, he found himself praying that the moon would not be long in rising. It was nearly midnight before that prayer was answered, and he had gone only halfway back to the spot where Gallup had pitched his camp. Once the moon rose above the horizon, he was able to pick up his pace. Since the moon was only partial, he saw little of the canyon off to his left except a yawning black scar in the earth. The ground around him was pale gray, but the contrast between earth and chasm was enough for him to move with confidence. He still had to be concerned about noise, and kept far enough away from the rim that no one below could see him.

When he reached the spot where Fallon and the others had pitched their camp, he could still see a faint flicker of light coming up from the canyon floor far below. He dismounted, walked to the rim, and peered over the edge. Brady could see the three men sitting around their fire. Judging by the movements of their heads, they were talking, but their voices were too soft for him to hear what was being said. There was no point in lingering, and the last thing he needed was to be spotted. If they saw him now, his plan, such as it was, would be worthless. For one brief instant he thought about opening fire from the rim, but the thought of such cold-blooded murder made him cringe. Instead, he backed away from the rim, grabbed the chestnut by the reins again, and jerked them hard, as if to punish the horse for his own inability to act.

It was another hour and a half before he noticed the ground beginning to slope downward, gently at first, then more steeply. He wanted to be on level ground before daybreak, and he had to find someplace to hole up, someplace that he could defend but that would offer him a good vantage point from which to confront Gallup when he made his move.

By four A.M., he had managed to reach the flats at the opposite end of the canyon. He mounted the chestnut, trying to ignore how tired he was and how exhausted the horse had to be, and nudged him forward into the canyon mouth. He knew how far away the camp was, knew that he had nearly a mile in which to find the ideal spot for what he planned. It was four-thirty, with the sky already beginning to brighten by the time he found it, a large wedge-shaped niche in the wall, its narrow mouth offering access to a rather spacious triangular chamber. It offered excellent cover and a perfect view of a bend in the canyon. The angle gave a clear look at the entire width of the canyon without exposing him to anyone coming through from the far end.

He tugged the horse in, thought about removing its saddle, then changed his mind. He wanted to be ready to move at a moment's notice, and the chestnut would just have to endure the saddle for another few hours.

He sat down to wait, watching the sky above him turn milky gray and the last few stars disappear one by one. As he contemplated the coining confrontation, he found it harder and harder to think about opening fire without warning. Just as his hesitation on the rim had prevented him from pouring rifle fire down into the camp, his conscience was again starting to bother him. He didn't know whether he could ambush the three men. He'd already killed one man, a man he'd never met and as far as he knew had nothing against, and that fact was like an open sore. He kept trying to tell himself that it was the only way, that he could do it, that he had to do it and that Gallup and the others deserved no better.

But as many times as he told himself, he still knew it was a lie. The man he'd killed had gone for his gun, and Brady had acted in self-defense. Opening up on three unsuspecting men, no matter who, was something else again. And by the time the first tinge of dark red hinted that the sun was on its way up, he was as confused as he'd ever been in his life. All he knew for sure was that Molly had been taken from him and that loss had somehow to be addressed. Just exactly how was something he hoped he would know before he had to act.

And the more he worried, the harder it became to decide.

The clatter of hooves on broken stone did not hold the answer, and as he peered out into the canyon, he saw the three men just rounding a bend in the wall, and he knew that he didn't have any idea what he was going to do.

20

GALVANIZED BY THE approaching hooves, Brady grabbed his Winchester, sprinted out of the crevice, and planted himself in the middle of the canyon floor. The sound was growing louder, but he still couldn't see the horsemen. He was conscious only of the brightening gray overhead, the looming walls, still wrapped in shadows but already turning red with the rising sun, on either side of him, and the rifle in his hands. His fingers curled around the barrel so tightly that he was afraid they had turned to stone.

He saw the first rider then, looking back over his shoulder at the men behind him. Brady brought the rifle up, aimed, and held his ground. The rider turned, the reins in his hand, and started to lash them against the side of his mount, but froze when he spotted the solitary figure standing there, blocking his way.

Everything seemed to slow down then. Brady saw the reins, impotent now, fall slowly toward the ground, the lash interrupted by the rider's sudden immobility. The horse plunged on and the rider's mouth opened. Brady heard a sound, a shout that seemed to come up out of the very ground, a deep unintelligible rumble that echoed off the canyon walls and was lost in the shadows. The remaining cowboys turned the corner, shapeless as unfinished statues, edges blurred in shade, rounded and shapeless.

"Hold it right there," Brady shouted, his voice sounding tinny and feeble to his own ears.

The lead rider, Jim Anderson, jerked the reins, and his horse skidded so abruptly to a halt that sparks flew from its hooves as they slid across broken rock. The following men nearly barreled into him, reining in their own mounts and shouting at Anderson to move.

Brady fired one shot, aiming high, and he heard the bullet spang off rock, then whine off into the distance. "Get down," Brady snapped.

"Brady," one of the men said, "what the hell is this?"

He recognized Cody Fallon's voice, and the youngest of the three cowboys nudged his horse forward two or three steps.

"You know damn well what this is, Fallon," Brady barked.

It was brighter now, the gray overhead a rich red. Ruby light spilled down into the canyon, cascading over the rocks of the western wall, leaving the eastern wall dark, the jagged end of broken rocks high on the stony face jutting out like the stumps of bloody fingers.

Anderson made a sudden move, and Brady without thinking, fired. The heavy .44 slug slammed into Anderson's thigh and the cowboy growled with pain. He jerked the reins of his horse and turned, but the movement startled the horse into a sudden buck, and Anderson pitched from the saddle, breaking his fall with both hands. He tried to crawl away as his horse cantered off.

Fallon jumped from the saddle. He was looking at Brady, his face stunned. "What the hell did you do that for?"

Brady laughed. "Like you don't know."

"What? Why? I *don't* know, dammit!"

"If you don't know, why did your friend pull a gun on me yesterday? Why did the three of you run?"

Fallon shook his head. His lips, unnaturally pink in the red light, trembled, and his eyes grew large with his effort to understand.

"Donny said . . ."

But Brady interrupted him. "I don't care what Donny said. You answer the question. Why did you run?"

Anderson was still trying to drag himself across the ground, leaving a bloody smear from his wounded thigh as he crabbed behind a slab of red rock. Brady tried to keep one eye on the wounded man and the other on Fallon and Gallup.

Fallon walked over to Anderson and knelt beside him, keeping his eyes on Brady, as if he feared being shot in the back.

"While you're there, get his pistol and toss it over here. Do it nice and slow, Fallon, or I swear to God I'll kill you."

Brady watched the young cowhand carefully as he leaned over, removed the Colt from its holster, grasped it by the barrel, and started to toss it. Brady moved to catch the gun as it tumbled end over end through the air. Gallup went for his gun at the same moment. Brady saw the movement out of the corner of his eye, and swung the Winchester around, but the Colt smashed into Brady's rifle. Gallup got off a shot, and Brady hit the dirt.

Fallon scrambled away, reaching for his own gun at the same time. Brady fired, but the shot went wide, and Gallup jerked the reins and spurred his horse. Fallon tried to get to his feet, and Brady fired once more after the fleeing Gallup, who leaped from his horse and tumbled in behind some rocks.

Brady got to his feet and ran toward the niche in the wall, as Gallup emptied his pistol. Bullets slammed into the rocks all around Brady, sending razor-sharp fragments scattering in every direction. Brady dove through the narrow opening just ahead of the last round from Gallup's Colt.

He got to his feet and moved back toward the opening just in time to see Gallup yank his rifle free and swat at the big black horse to send it farther back into the canyon.

"Come on, Cody, I'll cover you," Gallup hollered, levering a round into the chamber of his Henry. Brady saw Gallup aim, and ducked back. He heard the bullet ricochet off the opening into the notch, then footsteps as Fallon raced to join Gallup.

Brady dropped to his stomach and tossed his head aside. Lying flat, he was able to slide into the narrow opening, the Winchester extended ahead of him. Gallup fired again, high, not knowing where Brady was. Brady fired back, and saw Gallup wince as the bullet grazed his arm. He heard a yelp, and Gallup cursed at him.

"You sonofabitch, Brady, I'm gonna have your ass."

Brady answered with another round, but there was no target, and Gallup stayed low. Fallon had joined him, and the younger man moved a few yards to Gallup's right so they could alternate fire, keeping Brady guessing and pinned where he was.

Two shots rang out, the sharp reports like hand-

claps in the confined space of the canyon. One of
the bullets glanced off the opening over Brady's
head and grazed his horse. He heard the chestnut
nicker in pain, then the clatter of hooves as the
wounded animal tried to tear loose from its tether.

Two more cracks sent another pair of bullets
into the niche, and the startled chestnut bucked
and kicked, finally managing to tear the reins free
of the scrub. It reared high in the air as another
shot barked from Gallup's direction. The horse
plunged toward the opening, forcing Brady to roll
to one side to avoid being trampled.

As it burst through the notch and out into the
canyon, Gallup fired again. Brady heard the impact of the bullet and saw the horse stagger and go
down to its knees. Blood trickled down its side as
it tried to get up, and another shot slammed into
the chestnut's head, shattering the skull and driving it all the way down. Its legs twitched in a final
spasm, then it lay on its side.

Brady cursed softly. He was horseless now, and
the only thing he could think to do was retaliate in
kind. Gallup's horse was beyond him, its head lowered as it tugged at some grass a hundred yards up
the canyon, and Brady got to his knees, sighted in
on the glossy chest of the black stallion, and fired
twice. The horse went down without a sound, and
Brady saw Gallup get halfway to his feet as he
turned to see what had happened. Brady fired

again and saw the slash of white as the bullet grazed a rock just to Gallup's left, nicking the cowboy's hat as it passed.

"Somebody help me!"

It was Anderson. Brady could just barely make out the wounded man's back. He was pressed flat behind a slab of stone, the brim of his hat sailing like a shark fin on a stony sea.

"Cody? Help me, please. I'm bleedin' real bad."

"Mr. Brady?"

It was Fallon.

"Forget it, Cody. He stays where he is, unless you two come out with your hands up."

"But what for? We never did nothing to you."

Brady didn't answer. He couldn't fathom such a bald-faced lie. He tried to imagine the smirk on Gallup's face, and it made him furious. "Go to hell, Cody. Give up, or die . . . those are your choices."

"What kind of choice is that? Give up for what?"

"More choice than you gave my wife."

"I don't know what you're talking about. What do you mean, your wife?"

Once more, Brady chose not to answer. Fallon had to know what he was talking about. He wasn't going to utter those awful words, not even there where Brady himself might be the only one who heard them to walk away.

"Help me, Cody. Donny? Help . . ." Anderson's voice sounded weaker now, and Brady knew the man had been badly wounded. He didn't think the bullet had cut an artery, but there was a lot of blood on the ground where he had crawled for cover, its glistening sheen already beginning to fade as the sunlight crept down the wall of the canyon and turned the bright red to dark brown.

It went against his nature to let an injured man suffer, but the circumstances were such that he had no choice. He knew that if he tried to help Anderson himself, they'd kill him as soon as he showed himself. And if he let Fallon or Gallup go to Anderson's aid, he'd be giving up the only leverage he had. As it stood, his own horse was dead, and so was Gallup's. Anderson's was behind him, and as long as it stayed where it was, Brady might be able to get to it if he needed to. Fallon's horse was loose somewhere, so Anderson was in trouble no matter how you looked at it—four men and two horses, miles from the nearest help. And the nearest water.

Anderson would start to get thirsty soon from the loss of fluid, but Brady's canteen was on his horse lying out in the middle of the canyon where he couldn't reach it without exposing himself to Gallup and Fallon's gunsights.

"Mr. Brady?" Fallon sounded tentative, even younger than he looked. Maybe it was the politeness of the address. Or maybe it was the fear in his voice that did it.

"What?"

"What did you mean before? About your wife, I mean?"

The question took him off guard. The words poured out of him then. "She's dead, Fallon, burned to death." It sounded like such a simple thing. Then, as if to clarify things, he added, "In a fire that you and your buddies started."

"What?"

"You heard me."

"But I didn't . . ."

"Shut up, Cody," Gallup barked. "He's lying."

Fallon ignored his partner. "I swear to God, Mr. Brady, I don't know anything about it."

"Just like you don't know what happened to Wes Fraser, is that it? People die all around you, and you don't see a goddamned thing. How convenient."

"I swear."

"I told you to shut up, Cody."

"Help me, somebody, please," Anderson croaked. The wounded cowboy's voice was even weaker now, and Brady found himself feeling remorse.

"Enough of this shit," Gallup snarled. A flurry of gunshots poured into the notch, and the ricochets swarmed around Brady's head like irritated bees. He pressed himself into the ground so hard he could feel the grit against his cheek, the sharp edge of a rock break the skin. Blood began to ooze from the puncture, and Brady felt it spread under the compressed flesh of his cheek.

Brady looked at the back wall of the notch, wondering if there was any way he could get out without being seen. The surface of the wall was uneven, outcrops studded it here and there, and there were slots where other pieces of the layered stone had pulled free. He might be able to climb, but he wouldn't get far before Gallup and Fallon could see him, and with his hands occupied, he'd be helpless. He sucked in his breath, then let it out in one long, exasperated hiss.

He had to think of something to break the deadlock. When the sun was higher in the sky, the canyon floor would be like an oven. Without water, and all but sleepless for two days, Brady knew he was on the edge of a precipice. If he didn't do something soon, he would get careless.

And that would get him killed.

21

THE HOURS DRAGGED ON. Anderson had stopped calling for help. Now, only an occasional moan came from behind the stone slab where he lay. Brady's throat was dry and scratchy. His tongue felt like a razor strop, and his lips were thick and stiff. He tried to stay out of the sun, but there was no doubt in his mind that he would have to make a move and make it soon. He was so thirsty, the only relief he got was from closing his eyes, and he knew that if he did that too often, one time he would drift off to sleep, and once Fallon and Gallup realized that, he would be a goner.

Twice, Gallup tried to sneak over to his own horse for a canteen, and Brady narrowly missed him. Then, to put a stop to it, he sighted in on the canteen, just visible alongside the crumpled stirrup of the dead black, squeezed the trigger easily, hold-

ing his breath, and was rewarded by the dull plink
of the slug slamming into the canteen. He saw a
spurt of water and a small geyser arcing away in
the sunlight, and fired again as Gallup cursed in-
coherently. The second bullet found its mark, and
Brady saw the canteen bounce away to lie in the
dust. He smiled to himself, imagining he could
hear the gurgle of the last of the water as it drained
from the riddled canteen and seeped into the dirt.

His own canteen lay on the ground, protected
from Gallup and Fallon by the carcass of the chestnut. It looked as if the horse had already begun to
stiffen and bloat, but he kept telling himself it was
just his imagination. He tried to tell himself the
same thing about his thirst, but his body wasn't
buying it. He also needed to get to his saddlebags,
where his extra ammunition was. His gunbelt was
full, but the .44 shells were the lighter loads intended for the Colt, and to make sure his rifle fire
was accurate at long range, he was going to need
to get to the box of heavier charges in the bags.

Once, he grabbed a rock the size of his fist and
threw it in the general direction of the cowboys. It
landed with a thud, then rolled a few feet, clinking
against the stones, but did not provoke a gunshot.
Brady was tempted to think he might be able to get
to the horse without drawing fire, but deep down,
he knew better. And getting there was only half the
problem. Getting back would be harder, because

they'd know which way he had to go once he broke from behind the carcass.

Or would they?

He spent the hour between two and three in the afternoon studying the distribution of large rocks in his immediate vicinity. More than a dozen were big enough to conceal him, provided he kept to a crouch and didn't get careless.

Brady was also concerned about Cody Fallon's horse. The big roan was drifting aimlessly in no-man's land. Two canteens hung from its saddle horn, and if he could get to the horse, or at least get the water, he'd have the upper hand. He'd already made up his mind to shoot the horse if he had to, but as long as it stayed well away from Fallon and Gallup, there was no need. For the better part of two hours, the roan had been a lot closer to Brady than to its owner.

The odds were long but, determined to make a try for his own canteen, which was only fifty feet away, Brady rolled on his belly and took a look at Gallup's position. He could just make out the cowboy's eyes below the brim of his hat. He was watching but didn't seem genuinely alert. A surprise dash might get Brady to the dead chestnut, but once he got there, what next?

Brady licked his lips, knowing that the answer didn't matter. He had to try it. To make the trip easier, he propped the Winchester against the inner lip of the niche opening, got into a crouch out of Gallup's line of sight, and pulled his Colt from its holster.

He counted to himself, resolved to make his break on three. One . . . two . . . three . . . and his knees were pumping almost before he realized it. He kept his eyes on Gallup as the cowboy jerked his head in surprise, then saw the barrel of a rifle come up over Gallup's cover. Thumbing back the hammer, Brady fired once, then again, and saw Gallup's hat disappear, and then he dove through the air. He landed just a couple of feet from the dead horse, scrambled like a terrified crab, and heard a bullet slam into the ground just inches from his feet. Instinctively, he doubled his legs, hauling them in and laying on his side. Listening for footsteps, he quickly jerked his canteen free and looped the leather strap around his neck. Opening the saddlebags, he groped inside until he found the box of rifle rounds, crammed it inside his shirt, then swiveled on the ground until he was back facing the niche again. But this time, he couldn't get a running start.

Brady cracked the Colt open, ejected the two spent rounds, fumbled two new shells into the cylinder, closed it, and thumbed the hammer back. The horse wasn't tall enough to cover him in a crouch, so he spun around again, crossing his fingers that his plan would work. Then, Colt in hand, he leaped to his feet as if he intended to run to the far wall, knowing that Gallup and Fallon would be expecting him to take the shortest route back to cover.

He saw Gallup trying to aim the Henry, but the gamble had worked, and Brady fired two quick shots, not caring whether he hit anything, as long as Gallup had to duck. For good measure, on a dead run, the canteen flapping against his hip, he fired in the general direction of Cody Fallon. Then he spun a hundred and eighty degrees and dashed back toward his cover. With less than fifteen feet to go, Brady stopped, gripping the Colt in both hands, hoping Gallup would show himself.

The cowboy, not realizing Brady was waiting for him, leaped to his feet, and Brady fired, but his shot was low, slammed into the stone slab, and sent Gallup sprawling headlong. Brady dashed the rest of the way home, panting, his parched throat threatening to close on him. He sprawled back into the niche, wrestled the cap off the canteen, and filled his mouth with the tepid water. He knew better than to gulp the water down, and waited until the dehydrated tissues of his mouth and throat had recovered a little before permitting himself a small swallow.

Hot, bitter with the taste of sunbaked metal, it still tasted as good as water dipped from a mountain stream. He filled his mouth again, swirled the

water around, fighting the temptation to laugh out
loud, and downed the mouthful in a single swallow. Reluctantly, he screwed the lid back on, set
the canteen on the ground, and crawled back to
the opening.

Gallup was nowhere to be seen. Not even his hat
showed. He could make out the dusty crown of
Cody Fallon's black Stetson, but the older man
seemed to have vanished. Brady listened intently—
for footsteps, the crack of one rock on another, the
creak of leather, the jingle of spurs—but heard not
a sound. Nevertheless, he was convinced that Don
Gallup had made a move. Out of water, his hand
had been forced. He was out there somewhere, not
a hundred and fifty yards away, and Brady, like a
goddamned fool, had managed to lose him in
broad daylight.

Taking a deep breath, Brady grabbed the Winchester and the canteen, looped the leather swtrap
around his neck again, and moved deeper into the
niche. Slipping the Winchester through his belt, he
used handholds to haul himself up the wall a few
feet, then spread-eagled, he reached as far as he
could with his left foot to get a toehold on a large
boulder forming one wall of the niche. It was a delicate balance, and he rocked back and forth a couple of times to get enough momentum to swing his
weight out over the boulder before bringing his
right foot across the gap.

He nearly lost his purchase as his left foot gave
way, and landed hard on the knee, but managed to
sprawl forward until his slide was arrested. Claw-
ing with both hands, he pulled himself atop the
boulder, then got to his knees. He could nearly see
over the niche wall nearest to Gallup's last position. Getting to his feet, he crouched down behind
a flat slab of red rock. Its edges crumbled as he
brushed against them, but he could see clearly
now, and spotted Cody Fallon's hat and part of the
young cowboy's shoulder.

There was still no sign of Don Gallup, and
Brady knew it was time to shove all his chips into
the pot. He crawled atop the slab and lay flat on
his back, pulled the Winchester free, then rolled
over. At the same instant, he heard footsteps below
him and leaned out to look over the edge. He
found himself staring down at the top of Gallup's
head. The cowboy must have heard something, because he glanced up and shouted, "Cody, get him!"

As Brady tried to bring the Winchester into firing position, it banged against the rock and slipped
from his grasp, sliding over the edge and down to
the ground fifteen feet below him. He grabbed for
his Colt as Gallup pounced on the rifle and started
to back away, his own Colt staring at Brady with
its single black eye.

Brady saw the flame and ducked, then heard the
crack, all the while thinking that he'd been hit,

thinking that the bullet must have struck him even before he saw the flash. But nothing happened. The whistle of the bullet, just inches high, died away as Brady found Gallup in his sights and squeezed the trigger. The heavy Colt bucked in his hand, and he thumbed the hammer back and squeezed again, remembering what it had felt like to hold the pistol after so many years, staring down the barrel at a sheet of paper with circles penciled on it.

He saw the front of Gallup's shirt puff out, a black hole at the center of the bulge in the cloth, then saw the black hole turn red as Gallup staggered backward, the pistol already slipping from his unclenching hand. The gun dangled for a moment, the weight of the barrel pulling it down, pivoting it in Gallup's trigger finger.

As Brady saw Fallon stand up, he pitched himself forward off the rock, landed hard on his shoulder, and rolled over. Pain flashed like prairie fire the length of his right arm as he scrambled to get to his Winchester. He saw Gallup fall, his eyes locked on Brady's, his mouth a twisted smile. A small bubble of blood engorged on Gallup's lips and burst with a brilliant flash, and the cowboy fell on his side.

Brady snatched at the rifle, snagged it by the barrel, and got to his feet, bent at the waist to keep his profile small. He kept telling himself to run, and his legs seemed for the longest time to refuse. Then one foot rose out of the dust and moved slowly forward. The other foot followed, and Brady turned the corner, feeling his spine curl like an armadillo's, shrinking away from the impact he knew must surely come.

But he was behind the rock now, and nothing had happened. He'd made it, and now only Cody Fallon stood between Brady and his children. He lay there panting, feeling his heart pounding, the tiredness squeezing every bone in his body.

For a moment, he didn't realize that Fallon was calling to him. When the voice finally registered, it sounded closer than it should have, and he sprang to his feet, pushing away the exhaustion one more time. He had the rifle in his hand as he pressed his back against the rocks, and the words started to sink in.

"Mr. Brady, I'm coming over there. Mr. Brady? Can you hear me? Are you all right?"

"Fallon," he rasped, "you come close and I'll kill you. You hear me? Gallup's already dead. We both know that. And you're next."

"I don't care what you say, Mr. Brady. I'm coming. Here, here's my guns." Brady heard the clatter of metal on stone and saw a Colt pistol land in the dirt a few feet from the opening. Fallon grunted then, and a rifle landed beside the Colt. "I don't have any weapons, Mr. Brady. As God is my witness, I don't have any weapons."

Brady was confused. The kid sounded like he was telling the truth, but the hot metal in Brady's gut was still there. He still felt empty except for its searing heat.

"I . . . I'm sorry about Mrs. Brady. But I promise you, I didn't know anything about it. Honest to God, I didn't."

"You and your friends killed Molly," Brady said, his voice rising to a howl. "You killed her."

"No! Not me. I swear. I didn't know about the fire."

"You expect me to believe that?" Brady stepped into the open then, the rifle held in front of him, his finger on the trigger. The gun was cocked, and his finger trembled against the hot metal.

He saw Fallon then, standing there with his hands high in the air. Fallon's hat was pushed back on his head, and he looked so incredibly young. Brady felt the weight of the past few days as if each one had aged him a decade.

"I'm going to get some water now, and see if I can save Jimmy. I don't care what you do, Mr. Brady. You want to shoot me in the back, you go right ahead and do it, but I got to get him some water. If he ain't already dead."

With that, the kid turned on his heel and started to walk back toward his horse, keeping his hands high, where Brady could see them. "Wait," Brady said. "Here . . ." And when Fallon turned, Brady tossed him his canteen.

Fallon nodded as he snatched at the canteen, turned again, and walked over to the slab of stone behind which Jim Anderson still lay. He had already unscrewed the lid, and knelt down beside the wounded cowboy. Brady stood over him and watched as Fallon cupped his friend's head in one hand and held the canteen to Anderson's lips with the other.

"Come on, Jimmy, wake up. You got to wake up," he said.

Anderson had stopped bleeding, but his left thigh was caked with clotted blood, and his face was pale under a range tan. His eyes were motionless, his lips almost white. Brady thought for sure he was dead.

But Fallon refused to give up. He squeezed Anderson's cheeks, pinching them to try to wake him. With a thumb, he felt for a pulse, and looked up eagerly when he found one. "He's alive," he said. "I knew it. He's alive."

Anderson groaned then, and his eyelids flickered momentarily.

"Drink, Jimmy," Fallon said, tilting the canteen. Water trickled from its mouth and down over Anderson's chin. Then his mouth opened, and he sucked greedily at the trickle until Fallon forced the mouth of the canteen between his lips.

"Not too much, Jimmy," Fallon said. Then, pulling the canteen away, he said, "There's more, but I got to know something first."

Anderson nodded that he understood.

"What happened with Mr. Fraser? Did you shoot him?"

Anderson shook his head. "Donny," he croaked.

"Is it true, what Mr. Brady said? Did you and Donny set fire to his barn?"

This time Anderson nodded.

"Donny done it," Anderson said. "We was trying to get even with him for testifying against you."

Fallon looked up at Brady then, his eyes suddenly moist. "I'm sorry," he said. "God, I'm so sorry."

Brady nodded dumbly, closed his eyes and squeezed them tight, feeling the tears seep through the lids and trickle down over his cheeks. Sorry didn't change things, he thought. But it was all he was going to get.

Opening his eyes, he nodded. "Yeah," he said. He lowered the rifle then, as if the weight of it had finally defeated him, and let it fall to the ground. He sat down, leaned back against the rock, and closed his eyes once more.

Catch the riveting new hardcover from
New York Times bestselling author Tony Hillerman
as Leaphorn and Chee join forces to solve a
puzzling new mystery, from the discovery of a
murdered man with no ID to covert activities
on a big game ranch.

TONY HILLERMAN
THE SINISTER PIG

ISBN: 0-06-019443-X
Price: $25.95/NCR

Available wherever books are sold
or call 1-800-331-3761 to order.

🎞 HarperCollins*Publishers*
www.harpercollins.com
SP 0603